THE ACCIDENTAL ADVENTURES OF ONION O'BRIEN

—

THE SECRET SCIENTIST

JASON BYRNE

ILLUSTRATED BY OISÍN McGANN

GILL BOOKS

Gill Books
Hume Avenue
Park West
Dublin 12
www.gillbooks.ie

Gill Books is an imprint of M.H. Gill & Co.

Edited by Oisín McGann
Printed by ScandBook in Lithuania

This book is typeset in Nimrod.

The paper used in this book comes from the wood pulp of managed forests. For every tree felled, at least one tree is planted, thereby renewing natural resources.

A CIP catalogue record for this book is available from the British Library.

5 4 3 2 1

TO THE BEST GRANDADS, DADS AND HUSBANDS EVER: MR EDDIE McCREITH AND MR PADDY BYRNE. WE MISS YOU SO MUCH. THANKS FOR ALL THE LOVE AND LAUGHS YOU GAVE US, AND ARE STILL GIVING US IN OUR MEMORIES.

CHAPTER ONE:
—
THE DRONE WITH A MIND OF ITS OWN

As usual, it was all going wrong for Onion. Clíona had shown him how to use her phone to control the drone that flew overhead, but it wouldn't do what it was told. It was spinning and swooping all over the place, its four electric motors buzzing at a high pitch as it smacked through the foliage of one of the trees about fifty metres away.

'Hey, take it easy, Onion!' Clíona said. 'You'll crash it if you keep doing that.'

'It's not me – I'm doing what YOU said!' he gasped in frustration.

'Well, obviously you're *not*,' she replied.

'He's totally gonna crash it,' Sive said, folding her arms.

The others nodded in agreement. It was Saturday morning, and they were out on the rough grass of the local bit of waste ground known as the Valley, not far from their school. They'd all taken a turn at flying Clíona's new drone, and finally it had come to Onion's go. Now they were all nervous. Onion could barely get his body to move the way he wanted; they could only imagine what he'd do with a complicated remote-control aircraft.

Part of this lack of coordination was because of his wonky eye, which meant that he had to wear glasses and an eye patch. The patch covered up his *good* eye to make the wonky one work harder, so it would look in the direction it was supposed to. A lazy eye, the doctors called it. Onion never understood why – it wasn't like it refused to get up for school each day: it was a bloody eye. He couldn't blame it all on his eye, though – mostly, Onion was just 'all fingers and toes', as Granny Mary would say, or 'has wet bread for fingers', as Grandad Paddy would say, which made no sense at all.

Top 5 Reasons for Onion's Eye to Go Wonky Then Straight Again

1. Wonky: When he hears a wolf howl.
   Straight: When he realises it's a dog.

2. Wonky: When he hears a Banshee scream in the night from a misty hill.
   Straight: When he realises it's just a fox running out of the forest.

3. Wonky: When he sneezes.
   Straight: When he sneezes (he literally sneezes it back straight).

4. Wonky: When an arm suddenly lands on his shoulder in the dark.
   Straight: When he realises he's just backed into Granny Mary's coat rack.

5. Wonky: When a girl says 'Hi'.
   Straight: When a girl says 'Bye'.

'Have a bit of faith, guys,' Dallan said. 'He'll get the hang of it.'

Dallan had worse eyesight than Onion, but much more stylish glasses, and he squinted through them as the dot veered towards the sun. Then the drone flew over the treeline and disappeared from sight. They heard the buzzing fade into the distance.

'Ah, Janey.' Clíona sighed, snatching the phone from Onion.

'Told you so,' Sive said, putting a stick of gum in her mouth and starting to chew.

'Oh, you are such a guzzer,' Dallan said to his mate.

'It's not my fault!' Onion whined.

Sive O'Connor, Dallan Okoye, Clíona O'Hare and Onion O'Brien were the four core members of the gang they called the Five O's. Derek, Onion's older brother, was officially the fifth member, but he always objected to being included, saying he wasn't part of 'their stupid gang'. Today, they were out testing the drone, which was a mongrel piece of electronics Clíona had made from the wreckage of drones they'd found lying around the Valley.

CHAPTER ONE: THE DRONE WITH A MIND OF ITS OWN

The local teenagers were always flying, and crashing, them around there.

'Hang on,' Clíona said. She was rubbing her fingers around the screen of her phone, trying to take back control of the drone. She could also use the screen to see through the drone's camera. 'I think maybe it *wasn't* Onion's fault. Something funny's going on here. I can't get it to respond. It's doing its own thing.'

'Maybe it's getting too far away for the signal to reach,' Sive suggested, running her hands through her dark, spiked hair. 'Or, y'know, it just didn't want to listen to Onion.'

They all looked towards the trees where the drone had disappeared, and then they started running. Jumping the stream that ran the length of the Valley, they then followed a path that led through the trees and out the other side, through a bit more rough ground covered in tufts of grass and brambles. They bolted across this small clearing full of trip hazards just in time to see the drone fly through the trees ahead and vanish over a high wall.

Now, even though they couldn't see it, they could still hear it, its motors constantly changing pitch as if it was changing direction over and over again. Sive and Dallan, who were the fastest runners, reached the wall and looked around for a way to climb over. By the time Onion and Clíona arrived, the first two had found an old oak whose lower branches offered a view over the wall. Sive was already up there and

CHAPTER ONE: THE DRONE WITH A MIND OF ITS OWN

Dallan was waving to the others to go ahead of him. Despite being pretty athletic, he was always cautious when it came to climbing, on account of the care he took with his designer clothes.

Clambering up the knotty wood, they all sat astride the branch with the best view and gazed out over the wall. Beyond it lay the grounds of some large building, three storeys high and surrounded by a garden dotted with bushes and hedges and concrete paths.

'This is ... hang on, I know this place,' Onion said. 'This is the back of the old folks' home, St Brigit's of the ... whatchamacallit ... the Weeping Wound. Candy Dan's gran lives here now. And Mrs Toadstool from down the road.'

'You mean Mrs Tattle,' Dallan corrected him.

'*Tunstall*,' Sive said. 'Her name's Mrs *Tunstall*. Anyway, what's the deal with the drone?'

'It's there, look.' Clíona pointed.

They all stared. The drone was doing aerobatics over the garden, incredible manoeuvres, sweeping down low, then climbing and curving up into a loop, then flipping into barrel rolls and tumbles.

'I didn't know it could even do stuff like that,' Clíona said, gaping at the sight.

'Maybe it's like in *Terminator*. The machines are coming alive,' Dallan said.

'Don't be a complete wall-starer, Dallan,' Sive said. 'The machines are not coming alive. And if they were, they wouldn't start with Clíona's drone. They'd take over a … I don't know, something useful like a stealth bomber.'

'How do we know they haven't done that too,' Dallan retorted, 'if it's a *stealth* bomber?'

Everyone glanced up at the sky for a moment, wondering.

'What is a stealth bomber? It sounds like something Grandad travelled to work in when he was younger,' Onion said.

'Oh, it's a very, very skinny plane that can hide from radar, so it's a …' Clíona stopped explaining to Onion as she watched his wonky eye turn in with all the confusion.

'Anyway, Ballinlud is too boring to bomb,' Sive said.

'No, this is something else,' Clíona insisted. Her long hair hung over the sides of her face as she looked down at her phone. She could still see through the camera, but the controls didn't work at all. Someone else was controlling the aircraft. 'What is going on?'

'There's someone out there,' Dallan said. 'Look, near the door.'

Sure enough, an old man was sitting on a bench near the back door of the home. A frail figure in rumpled clothes, he had a tablet and was holding it up, moving his thumbs over it. His eyes were flicking between the drone and his screen.

'That's Pixel Pat!' Sive exclaimed. 'He was that champion game player on all those clunky games back in the eighties. He used to run the games arcade in the shopping centre. I heard they had to put him in a home because he'd gone a bit dotty. So this is where he ended up.'

'Has he … has he *hacked my drone*?' Clíona said in disbelief. 'No way has he done that! You just messed with the wrong aircraft, mister! Dude, you are going *down*!'

The others looked at their friend in surprise. Clíona was normally a very gentle soul, the quiet one in the group, who preferred books to people, and games and inventions over the real world. Now, her whole body was tensed under the loose shirt and combats she always wore. Scrunching up her face, she opened up a new window on her screen and started tapping something in.

Onion, who was closest to the trunk of the tree, heard a soft cracking sound and looked around. 'Guys, I think we've got another problem here …' he said.

'He's awesome at flying that thing,' Sive was commenting. 'Maybe we could just watch for a bit?'

'Guys?' Onion groaned.

There was another crack. The branch sagged, ever so slightly.

'Clíona's on the warpath here,' Dallan replied. 'She's about to unleash a nerd-whuppin' on that guy. He's gonna get hacked to the max, am I right, Clee?'

'YOU MESS WITH THE BEST, YOU DIE LIKE THE REST!' Clíona snarled.

'You tell 'im, girl.'

'Guys,' Onion said more urgently, 'I think we need to –'

The branch snapped. There was a terrible moment of weightlessness, and they all crashed down into the bushes on the other side of the wall. The heavy branch bounced off the wall and nearly thumped them across the heads before it flopped forward onto the grass. Dragging themselves out of the bushes, they cast their eyes around and realised they were in the garden of the old folks' home, with no way to climb back out over the high wall. Dallan groaned at a new stain on his trousers.

'And who do we have here?' a voice asked in an imperious tone. The four Five O's turned to see a man stepping out from behind a large bush with a petrol-powered hedge trimmer in his hands. He was wearing a hands-free headset for a phone. He spoke into it: 'Adrienne, call the guards. Looks like we have ourselves some intruders on the grounds.'

CHAPTER TWO: — TAKING FLIGHT

For a moment, the four Five O's stood frozen by the sight of the dour man with coiffed hair, a little moustache and his trimming appliance. But this paralysis only lasted long enough for their brains to reboot after the fright.

'RUN!' Sive roared.

And they ran.

Unfortunately, none of them knew which way to run, and they weaved around until eventually splitting up and running in two different directions. There were walls and hedges dividing up the grounds and joining the walls of the building, so Onion aimed for the only escape route he could see:

the back door that stood ajar, a few metres from where Pixel Pat was slouched on the garden bench.

Pixel, who'd been giving his full attention to the drone, looked up at Onion and blinked, shaking his head, as if he was waking up from a nap. Then he gazed blearily at the tablet in his hand as if he didn't know what it was. Onion was running towards him when the drone came whining down out of the sky, heading straight for Onion's head. He squealed, but Dallan leaped up behind him and snatched the thing from the air before it could hit him. Switching off the power, Dallan let the rotors stop spinning and then tucked the drone under his arm.

The two boys barrelled through the door and found themselves in a hallway. Through another door, they saw a kind of lounge full of old people in chairs and sofas and wheelchairs, all facing the same direction. It was like Mass, but with soft furnishings.

'Follow my lead. Act casual,' Dallan said, striding confidently into the room.

He then proceeded to act anything but casual, whistling as he swaggered through the room full of old people, all of them watching the telly. He was winking at some of the ladies, clicking his tongue and pointing pistol-hands at some of the men, throwing in some dance moves and generally behaving like someone who has never acted casual and has no idea how it's supposed to look.

'Don't mind us, folks, we're just passing through. Visiting our grandparents. You keep doing your thing. Love that dress, ma'am! Is that a new colour in your hair? Are you just back from a facial? What are *you* doing in here – you're far too young for this place!'

'Hello, Onion!' a woman called out, and Onion turned to recognise Mrs Tunstall, who had once lived down his road. She had a slightly flattened, smiley face perched on a pile of hand-knitted clothes. Her permed hair formed a wide, helmet-like cap over her head, which had inspired the nickname the kids in the area sometimes used for her, 'Mrs Toadstool'. Before she'd moved out of her house, Mrs Toadstool had been the nosiest neighbour on the road. Onion's grandad and other grown-ups had a different nickname for her: they called her 'Mrs Tattle'.

'Howaya, Mrs Ta– Toa– Tunstall!' he said, cringing. Because *of course* the nosey woman knew who he was and would be able to identify him to the guards. 'How's it goin'? Good?'

'Oh, can't complain. Getting my feet done on Friday.'

'That's … nice.'

'They need doing, can't let the feet go undone.'

'Oh, the feet, never. I'd better be off.'

'All right then. Say hello to your granny for me – tell her I'll be over to show her me new feet.'

'I will, of course. Look after your feet there, then … eh …' His wonky eye was losing the plot now.

'WOW, those dentures make you look like a Kardashian!' Dallan was still working the crowd as he walked. 'And nice wheels! Is that a motorised wheelchair? Wicked! How are *you*, sir? That is a magnificent moustache … sorry, I mean nostril hair. Is this the way out? Thanks, everyone, it's been emotional. See y'all now!'

Some of the old people responded to Dallan's enthusiastic greetings and seemed happy to see a couple of new faces, but others just sat with glassy eyes and dull expressions, as if they weren't quite there any more. Onion couldn't bring himself to match Dallan's lively banter.

'You're some eejit,' he said, as they hurriedly pushed through the door into another hallway, with the front door ahead of them.

'What? We made it, didn't we?' Dallan shrugged.

'Yeah, yeah, *we made it*.' Onion took a moment to take a drag on his inhaler, which his granny made him keep on a cord around his neck. His nerves wouldn't be right for hours.

'Hold it right there!' It was the man with the hedge trimmer, though he no longer held the hedge trimmer. With powdery white skin and a flushed, pointy face, he was holding up his phone now, trying to get a picture of them. 'Don't you move, you little WRETCHES! You'll stop right there and wait for the guards, so you will!'

The two lads had other ideas, and they charged through the front door and down the driveway before he could focus on them. Sive and Clíona came scrambling over a low wall to their right and caught up, all four of them racing for the gate. They dodged around a powerful-looking motorbike and a couple of parked cars as they saw two other men in carers' uniforms coming at them from the left. Then they were at the gate, sprinting out onto the path that ran along the road.

CHAPTER TWO: TAKING FLIGHT

The two men were gaining on them, and the Five O's, gasping for breath, found themselves sprinting down the main road that led to Dundeer, the next suburb over. Just down the road was an arcade of shops that included a newsagent, a Chinese takeaway and the salon where Onion's Granny Mary got her hair done, The Hair-Do or Dye.

It was pretty typical of Onion's luck that, just as the men were making their rude gestures at the children, Granny happened to come out of the salon with her freshly done and dyed tower of fox-brown hair. Given the choice between being dragged to the guards by the two guys or being saved by his granny, Onion would have needed some time to think it over. As it was, his fate was sealed in the next few seconds.

'Onion O'Brien, what in God's name is going on here?' she called out. The four kids faltered, their hearts seized in fear as Granny's mammy voice went from 'suspicious' to 'fully armed'. 'What have you been doing this time?'

'They've been *trespassin'*, missus!' one of the carers called after them, catching up now that that the children were slowing down. 'Scared some of our residents! You can't be doing that ...'

He was a Filipino lad, but the mammy voice knows no borders. Every country has their own version. The kids could see his eyes widen in fright as he found himself in the full glare of Granny's fury. It was like watching a man run into a sandstorm. His mate had already stopped and was hanging back a few metres, ready to turn around if a swift retreat was called for.

'What are you doin', chasin' after kids like that, frightening the bejayzuz out of them and everyone around them, including me?' Granny barked at the first guy, the lines going hard on her worn face. 'Sure, they're only little and you a grown man, charging at them like one of them bulls in ... Pamplova ... or Purplona or ... or ...'

'Pamplona,' the man offered, slowing to a stumble now. 'It's in Pamplona where they run the bulls through the town ...'

'Don't you talk back to me, young man. I know perfectly well where the bulls run in Pamplioima!

'I'm forty-three, missus.'

'Still young enough for a GOOD SLAP! I'll have no more of your cheek! Run off with you now, and don't be bothering my grandson and his friends. If they've been up to something, I'll deal with them. Go on, now! Don't think I won't call your mother if I need to.'

'Good luck with that. My mam lives in the Philippines.'

'Well, I'll slap you so hard, you'll end up beside her, Philip or no Philippines!'

The man was about to say something else, but then decided he was outgunned and took a few steps backwards before turning and hurrying away. Onion swallowed hard, trembling as he hid behind his granny. Sive was grinning.

'Thanks, Mrs O'Brien! That was–'

'Don't thank me, Sive O'Connor!' Granny turned on her, her finger pointing as if there was a laser coming out the end of it. 'Or any of the rest of you. Not another word for you lot. *Onion*, you're going to tell me what's been going on, and then I'll decide what I'm going to do with all of you. God in heaven, I just wanted a relaxing afternoon and to get my hair done and you've gone and got me all frazzled. I'll have to get a reset at this stage. Back to the house, the lot of you, before I post you all to the Philippines, or wherever it was, and leave you there!'

Facing the threat of being posted to the Philippines, the others all shut their mouths, dropped their eyes to the ground and started towards home, while Granny interrogated Onion.

She wasn't happy with what she heard.

CHAPTER THREE:
MAKING AMENDS

Granny was shocked that they'd trespassed in the old folks' home. Some of their former neighbours lived there, and she was mortally embarrassed that her grandson might have frightened some of the old dears. She was even more embarrassed that Onion had been spotted by Mrs Tattle, because it meant half of Ballinlud would know by the end of the day. She totally dismissed their excuse that Pixel Pat had hacked their drone – that made her all the more annoyed.

'Don't be talking nonsense,' she told them. 'Pat's got advanced Alzheimer's. He can't hold a thought in his head from one moment to the next. He couldn't hack a scone with a bread knife.'

They were sitting in the kitchen, where Granny had started baking buns. She'd decided to bring some to St Brigit's of the Weeping Wound that afternoon to 'make amends' for the kids' intrusion. 'Making amends' was just a posh way of saying sorry. Granny loved to think she was posh, but only on the phone or in front of other people. She'd already spoken to the parents of the other Five O's, and they'd agreed that all the children should join Granny on the visit. Onion's little sister, Molly, was 'helping' with the baking, which meant she'd stuck her fingers in both the icing bowl and her nose several times. Onion was trying to ice the buns while encouraging Molly to sneeze because she'd got icing stuffed up both nostrils.

Granny was putting another batch of buns in the oven when the power suddenly went off. She gave a sigh of frustration and checked the light switch.

'Granny, the 'lectric's gone!' Molly called out.

'Yes, love. For goodness' sake, not again. That's the fifth time this week – and the second time today!'

Upstairs, they heard some cursing and then the sound of feet clattering down the stairs. Derek burst into the kitchen. He was Onion's older brother, and officially he was the fifth of the Five O's, though he refused to be involved in their 'stupid gang'. From the horrified look on his face now, anyone might have thought he'd seen zombies thumping at the windows. The waft of Lynx Africa body spray billowed ahead of him as he came in and filled the space around him as he came to a stop.

'My hairdryer's not working!' he exclaimed.

'That's what happens when the power goes off,' Granny told him. 'Don't worry, I'm sure they'll have it sorted soon.'

'But I'm meeting the lads! It's Saturday! We're going to hang out at the shopping centre.'

'Can't you just let your hair dry naturally, love?' she asked.

'It won't keep its shape if I do that!' he whined. 'I just got this done.'

'Oh, me too,' she said, holding her hands up to her own do.

You might wonder why Onion and his brother and sister lived with their grandparents instead of their mother and father. The fact of the matter was their parents had disappeared some years before in mysterious circumstances.

But that is another story for another time.

'Well, you could just not go to the shopping centre and come to St Brigit's instead, if you like,' Granny offered.

'What's St Brigit's? Sounds like somewhere I'd end up smelling of disinfectant instead of me lovely Lynx Africa.' Derek sniffed his pits as he said this, though his tone suggested he had no interest in going anywhere that was named after a saint, as it might be some kind of school in disguise. Neither he nor Onion could ever understand why the government insisted on naming schools after saints.

Top 5 Worst Saints to Name Your School After

1. St Polycarp of Smyrna – patron saint of diarrhoea

2. St Julian the Hospitaller – patron saint of murderers

3. St Genesius – patron saint of clowns and torture victims

4. St Adrian of Nicomedia – patron saint of arms dealers

5. St Drogo – patron saint of unattractive people

'We're going to the old folks' home,' Onion said. 'We're bringing them buns.'

'And icing,' Molly added, still trying to clear her nostrils.

Derek looked genuinely baffled. 'Why ... why would I go to an old folks' home?'

'Because it's a nice thing to do?' Onion suggested.

'Oh, right, so that's why *you're* going, is it?'

'Well ... no. I have to say sorry for giving them all a fright, bursting in on them, because Pixel Pat hacked our drone.'

Derek scowled at him. 'Nothing you say ever makes any sense – you actually hurt my brain when you talk.'

It was at this moment that Grandad came in the front door. 'Power's out on the whole street – the Germans must be coming!' He laughed as he entered. 'Here, do I smell buns?'

'And icing!' Molly shouted to him, then she snorted and started coughing.

Grandad strode through to the kitchen, then

threw his jacket over the back of a chair and his newspaper on the table. He was a tall, limber man who still worked as a handyman, despite his age, and had been meeting his mates for lunch down the Ballinlud House every third Saturday for fifty years.

'You wouldn't believe what's been going on down the pub,' he said, shaking his head. 'I went in for a quiet bit of lunch and a game of darts and who do you think shows up?'

'I thought you were going for the paper?' said Granny.

'Ah, yes, the paper ... Well, the fella who sells the paper started selling them over the bar in the pub, so now, to my annoyance, I have to go to the bloody pub to get the paper,' explained Grandad.

'You should work for the newspapers with a story like that,' answered Granny.

'Ah, listen, will ye, woman – guess who showed up?' asked Grandad.

Who?' Granny asked, not because she wanted

to know, but because they'd been together so long, their conversations ran on automatic.

'Francie O'Halloran,' Grandad said. 'I thought he was dead. He wasn't. He's been up in that old folks' home these last four years. Would you believe it?'

'Sure, I've seen him up there loads of times,' Granny said. 'Who told you he was dead?'

'Nobody. We hadn't seen him in a while, so we just assumed,' Grandad replied, waving away this minor detail. 'But that's neither here nor there. Anyway, Francie comes in and challenges the *whole room* to a game of darts. Says he'll give fifty quid to anyone who can beat him. And, sure, who's going to say no to that? We all knew he was half-blind, wearing those glass bricks on his face half his life. Couldn't get a driver's licence or nothing. Poor beggar couldn't *see* the dartboard, let alone hit it. So five of us step up. And what happens?'

'I don't know. What happens?' Granny asked, spooning some more mixture into bun cases.

'He squints through those thick glasses, and on every round, he fires off those darts like they're … they're laser-guided or something. Bang, bang, bang! One hundred and eighty, *every time*. Mary, who gets a *full score* every time?'

'I don't know, love,' she replied, rinsing off the wooden spoon. 'That's shockin'.'

Onion, who was scraping the last of the icing out of the bowl, frowned and looked up. Here was another resident of St Brigit's who'd suddenly developed incredible abilities. Could that be a coincidence?

'I've never seen anything like it,' Grandad said, shaking his head. 'At least, not in a pub game. It's like he was in one of those silly comic-book films where they get superpowers.'

'It's only *darts*, love,' Granny said.

'I know, but still … Made us look like fools …' Grandad mumbled, as he clicked on the kettle to make a cup of tea. The afternoon's events had obviously been a bit much for him. But there was no electricity, so it didn't click.

'Ah, Janey, can't a man have a cup of tea in his own house?' he muttered. 'What's the world coming to – sure, we were better off with the fire as a cooker.'

'That was in your mother's house, love,' said Granny.

'Well, we'd be better off ripping out the cooker and getting a fire in the kitchen so I could boil me kettle and not worry about bleedin' power cuts …' Grandad mumbled.

'Want some icing, Grandad?' Molly said, holding a lump of it out to him on her finger.

'No thanks, sweetheart. Kind of you to offer, though. I'm on a diet.'

'Of biscuits and beer,' replied Granny.

The power came back on, and everyone gave a little cheer. Derek raced back upstairs to his hairdryer, Grandad put the kettle on and Granny put the next batch of buns in the oven. Molly pushed a chair up against the wall to click the light switch on and off. Onion was leaning back in his own chair, chewing on his lip. Maybe it *would* be a good idea to go back St Brigit's of the Weeping Wound.

Something was going on there, and the Five O's were going to find out what it was.

CHAPTER FOUR:
BURNING RUBBER

Not long after all the buns were ready, the other Five O's arrived, ready to serve their sentence: one visit to the old folks' home. Sive was putting a brave face on it, though Onion could tell from the way she was chewing her gum that she was on edge. She dreaded making small talk. Though Clíona was nervous, she was curious, too, to see what she could learn from this new experience. Dallan was actually looking forward to the chats, and Onion was keen to begin his investigation.

Once Granny had gathered her young charges, she set off for the bus stop, leaving Grandad to mind Molly. This usually meant that Molly could do pretty much what she liked while he read his newspaper. Like most people in Ballinlud, they lived on a street of identical semi-detached houses, surrounded by many more streets of very similar semi-detached houses. The nursing home was only three stops away on the bus, not much more than a ten-minute walk, but there were biscuit tins full of buns to carry, and Granny had a whole bag of other stuff with her too. She wouldn't say what was in the bag.

They had barely reached the bus stop when they heard the squeal of skidding tyres and the throaty roar of a motorbike, and sure enough, one came racing up the street. It rose up into a wheelie as it passed the bus stop, and the rider, who wasn't wearing a helmet, raised her hand in a wave. Onion gaped in disbelief as he recognised the woman. She seemed to pass in slow motion before him, a giddy smile on her face. Her permed hair formed a wide, helmet-like cap over her head, blowing in the slipstream as she sped past. He noticed an odd detail as she did so, the number 5 written in black marker on the wrist she'd raised up to wave.

It was *Mrs Toadstool*. Riding past at high speed. Doing a *wheelie*. On a *motorbike*.

It was the same bike that Onion had seen parked in the driveway of the old folks' home. He was guessing it wasn't Mrs Toadstool's. Granny and the four Five O's  stared after her as she disappeared around the corner. Even Dallan was rendered speechless. It was only then they heard the siren, and a garda car flew past in hot pursuit, its blue roof lights flashing. The children recognised two of the local guards, Garda Fergus Plunkett, known as 'the Ferg', and his partner, Garda Bridie Judge.

'Now, there's something you don't see every day,' Dallan commented, the first to recover his powers of speech. 'Mrs Tattle –'

'It's Mrs *Tunstall*, Dallan,' Granny corrected him.

'– Mrs Tunstall, of all people,' Dallan continued, without missing a beat. 'Who'd have thought she had it in her? Never figured her for a stunt motorcyclist.'

'Never knew the woman to ride anything faster than a bicycle in her whole life,' Granny said. 'Though there was that time she went out with Billy the Skid, back in the day. He was a bad influence, that lad. Still, it's no way to behave, flyin' around like a divil. I'd have thought she had more sense. I wish people would act their age!'

Top 5 Lads Who Were a Bad Influence, Back in the Day

1. Jackeen John – a clever and nasty piece of work, destined for a life of crime

2. Baddie Barry Dalton – the Butcher of Ballinlud. The worst bully in the area, but also a butcher

3. Billy the Skid – a daredevil biker who lived fast, died young and left a good-looking corpse … Unfortunately, that corpse was found in a flattened shopping trolley, after he'd tried to jump it over a moving train

4. Mitchin' Mick – always skiving off school to play snooker. Now a professional snooker player who also owns an educational supplies company

5. Grandad Paddy – a bit of a messer, but a good grandad

As if in defiance of Granny's words, Mrs Tunstall came screeching back around the corner, still riding like the divil and doing another wheelie as she shot past again, leaving a smell of burning rubber. This time, a black van came out of a side road and swerved in front of her. She hit the brakes to avoid running into the back of it, her back wheel lifting off the ground. As she did so, the van's back doors were thrown open, the vehicle's driver brought the vehicle to a sudden stop, and the old woman and the bike went crashing into the dark interior. Two men leaned out, grabbed the doors and slammed them shut.

Moments later, the garda car came round the corner, siren blaring, roof lights flashing, and drove straight past the mysterious van and on down the road. The van did a casual U-turn, pulled up at the bus stop and the tinted window on the passenger side slid down. A woman with a pale face and sunglasses leaned out. She had slick, short black hair and was dressed in a black suit, white shirt and black tie. She winked, smiled and put a finger to her lips. And then the van pulled away, heading on down the road, carrying away Mrs Toadstool and her motorbike.

'Oh. My. God!' Sive said, chomping on her chewing gum.

'That was AWESOME!' Dallan whooped.

'That was *weird*,' Onion said.

'Goodness' sake. Where has that bus got to?' Granny muttered.

Minutes later, the bus arrived. During the short journey, the kids pressed themselves against the windows, hoping to catch sight of the black van, but there was no sign of it. Onion told them about Francie O'Halloran, who wasn't dead and had shown up at the Ballinlud House to beat Grandad and his mates at darts. This, after Pixel Pat and his mad drone-hacking skills. Another old-age pensioner who lived at St Brigit's of the Weeping Wound and who seemed to have developed amazing new abilities.

'Maybe they're retired superheroes,' Dallan said. 'And they come out and blow off some steam from time to time.'

'Superheroes aren't real, love,' Granny assured him. 'It *is* strange, though.'

'It's just coincidence,' Sive insisted. She was always the hardest to convince of anything. 'It has to be. We've seen some weird stuff and we're connecting it up. There'll be a totally reasonable explanation, you'll see.'

'What about the guys in that van?' Onion asked. 'That was some real spy stuff they pulled. What was going on there?'

Things got even stranger when they walked up the driveway of St Brigit's of the Weeping Wound. There was the motorbike that Mrs Toadstool had been riding, right back where they'd seen it earlier. It was definitely the same one – Clíona confirmed the licence place. She was a hardcore nerd and tended to notice details like that. The bike had a few new dents and scratches. Onion held his hand close to the engine. It was still warm.

They were all staring at it as Granny walked up the wheelchair ramp towards the front door. Before she got there, it opened and the dour guy with the coiffed hair stepped out. His eyes narrowed when he saw the children.

'What are you–?' he started to say, but Granny cut him off.

'They've come to apologise, Austin,' she told him. 'They know they've done wrong. Children? This is Mr Austin Leary, the manager of the home.'

'Chief executive officer,' he corrected her. Then he glared at the kids. 'I am the CEO of St Brigit's of the Weeping Wound, part of the Final Rest Home franchise. So you've come to say sorry, eh? Well, you can start by stepping away from my motorcycle. Any one of you puts a scratch on that and you'll feel my foot on your backside.'

'Tell that to the old lady who was using it to do wheelies down the street a few minutes ago,' Sive told him, grinding her gum between her teeth. 'Do you kick old women as well, or is it just kids?'

'Inconceivable!' Leary snorted. 'That bike hasn't left that spot all day. Are you a bunch of liars as well as trespassers?'

'Now, both of you, less of that,' Granny said, wagging a finger at them. 'Austin, they've come to make amends. We've brought buns. And I thought I'd hold a dance class for the residents to brighten up their day. What do you think of that?'

'A dance class?' Leary grunted.

'A dance class?' Onion repeated in a worried voice.

'A dance class,' Granny said to the four Five O's, pulling an old ghetto blaster tape deck from the bag she was carrying. 'We're going to do a spot of *ballroom dancing*.'

'Ah, jaypers,' Onion groaned.

CHAPTER FIVE:
THE HOUSE OF ANCIENT SPIRITS

Granny's plan was for the four children to act as dancing partners for the old people who wanted to take part in the class. The fact that none of the Five O's had ever done any ballroom dancing was no problem at all; Granny would show them how, as she'd 'done a bit of dancing back in her younger days'. Onion hadn't been this embarrassed since she'd licked a tissue to clean his face in front of everyone in the schoolyard. And that was only a month ago.

Austin Leary led them through to the living room, where most of the residents were sitting watching television. There was no sign of Mrs Toadstool, although Pixel Pat was there, staring in the general direction of the television as if he wasn't quite sure where it was. Three of the residents showed an interest in a dance class, another man in a motorised wheelchair said he'd take part if he could do so sitting down, and two others nodded their heads enthusiastically and then almost immediately forgot and went back to staring at the television. The rest appeared to take no notice whatsoever of what was going on.

'You'll get no sense out of them until the programme's over,' Leary said. 'Actually, you'll get no sense out of half of them anyway. They're a sleepy lot. They're watching *Murder, She Wrote*, and they won't miss it for anything.'

From the way he talked about them, it didn't sound like the CEO of St Brigit's of the Weeping Wound cared much for the residents in his care. He probably felt the same way about his staff too – a few of them were around, though none of them seemed to want to be in the same room as their boss.

CHAPTER FIVE: THE HOUSE OF ANCIENT SPIRITS

There was little else in the room for the elderly residents to do except watch the telly, and even that was a battered old box with a black and white picture. It was even older than the telly Onion's granny and grandad had at home. He'd seen geeks on the web who hunted for tellies like this – they were the dinosaur fossils of the tech world. Clíona stared at it in wonder.

Looking around, Onion couldn't see any bookshelves or board games or a games console or anything else to relieve the boredom of being stuck there all day. The Filipino guy, whose name was Danilo, was sitting at a table with one woman, helping her with a jigsaw whose pieces were bent and peeling apart with use. Another lady sat alone at a table, playing Patience with a worn pack of cards. The furniture was tatty and cheap and the walls hadn't been painted in years. Faded old watercolour prints hung on the walls, and the whole place smelled of damp and disinfectant, with a faint hint of body odour. Onion had visited other nursing homes when their school choir did the rounds at Christmas, doing carol singing. None of them had been this miserable.

'It's like I can feel the life being sucked out of me,' Sive whispered to him.

'Don't be mean,' Onion murmured back.

'This *whole place* is mean,' she replied. 'I'm just trying to fit in.'

Leary sniffed and turned away, striding back to his office. Granny sat down in a vacant armchair and started chatting to the oul' fella beside her, who turned out to be Francie O'Halloran. He squinted at her through thick glasses, nodding cheerfully and gesturing with shaky hands. He didn't seem very aware of where he was. He was just happy to have someone talking to him. It was hard to believe this squinty, shaky-handed guy had trounced the best darts players in the Ballinlud House only hours before.

Dallan had got talking to one of the zoned-out women, which came as no surprise, as Dallan could get anyone talking. Like Francie, she seemed

delighted to have someone's attention. Clíona had her notebook out and was looking around and jotting things down, like a Ghostbuster in a house filled with ancient spirits – which it was, in a way. Onion wondered how many years of life there was in this one room. He decided he'd take the chance to poke around a little while Granny was setting up and Austin Leary was busy elsewhere.

A corridor led off the living room, through a dining room and on down to the bedrooms. In the dining room, another man in a wheelchair sat by the window. This chair wasn't motorised. There would have been no point, for though his washed-out blue eyes were open, the man appeared to be completely lifeless except for the gentle rise and fall of his chest as he breathed. Even so, Onion found himself stopping to look at him.

He wore a crumpled grey suit and tie and had a chunky steel digital watch on his left wrist, the type from the seventies or eighties, when state-of-the-art watches could still only show time, seconds and the date. But it was the scar on his face that was fascinating. Onion couldn't tell if it was from a bullet or a burn or what; he looked like a Bond villain. There was a small round mark on his right cheek, and the skin around it was rough and crinkled. The right eye was paler than the left, and Onion wondered if it was blind. He touched his own left cheek, below where the glasses and patch covered his good eye – the one that didn't swing all over the place.

CHAPTER FIVE: THE HOUSE OF ANCIENT SPIRITS

A plain black notebook was tucked between the man's thigh and the side of the chair. Onion was peering closer when the man's left eye moved suddenly, locking onto him. Neither his face nor his body moved, but that eye knew what it was doing. Onion's heart jumped and he held his hands up, stepping back quickly.

'Sorry. I'm sorry, I didn't meant to stare. **I'm so sorry!'** Onion's eye began to go wonky, and the more the old man's eye moved, Onion's eye seemed to follow it – it was like an eye-off.

'Don't be worrying about that fella,' a voice said from behind him. Onion spun around to find Danilo standing there, a small, slim man with a pressed down but sensitive face. The carer waved at the man in the wheelchair. 'That's Alexander. Not up to much, really. We do our best for him, but he hasn't got much left upstairs, God love him.'

He leaned in closer to the man in the wheelchair and spoke in a slow, loud voice. **'ALEX? MR YURYEV? ALEXANDER, IT'S ME, DANILO!**

THE BOY DOESN'T MEAN ANY HARM, ALEX! HE'S JUST CURIOUS – HE THINKS YOUR SCAR IS COOL!'

'It *is* a cool scar,' Onion admitted. 'Might be the coolest in all of Ballinlud.'

Top 5 Coolest Scars in Ballinlud

1. Alexander Yuryev's hole of unknown origin

2. Karl O'Dean's arm scars that he said he got from being fitted with a bionic arm (fell off tractor)

3. Matt Malcolm's bullet holes in the side of his body (keyhole rib surgery)

4. Grandad Paddy's chest surgery scars (has been known to go topless in the pub to prove it)

5. Carmel Curtain's crop-circle shape in the back of her head (mole-removal surgery)

'Yeah. Makes him look like a Bond villain or something,' Danilo said, echoing Onion's thoughts and nodding to himself as he regarded the scar.

'Nobody knows how he got it. Me, I think he was poked in the face with an electric wire. I'm not sure what an electrocuted face looks like, but it has to be something like that, right?'

'I dunno, I suppose,' Onion said quietly.

'Zapped his brain too, I'd say. That's why he's like this now. It's not dementia or Alzheimer's like the others, apparently. Something much more mysterious. He got his brain zapped – I'd put money on it.'

'Could be. Maybe. Who was … Who is he?' Onion asked.

'Alex?' Danilo screwed up his face. 'He's Russian. Worked in a factory back in the Communist days. Probably made tractors. That's the kind of thing they did in factories in Communist Russia.

Tractors and ... and ... I dunno. Bad clothes. And chunky digital watches. History was never my thing. He came to Ireland years back to, you know, live in the capitalist paradise. Not even sure how he ended up here, but here he is, and we'll keep him as happy as we can.'

'I'd better head back,' Onion said, pointing towards the living room. 'My granny wants us to dance with the old folks.'

'Yeah, you shouldn't be back here, really,' Danilo said. 'Privacy an' all that. Don't want Mr Leary getting mad at you again.'

'He's a piece of work, that Mr Leary,' Onion said.

'That's one way of putting it.' Danilo grunted. 'He's a miserable git. Never kind to the folk here. The only thing he cares about is that motorbike of his.' He caught himself and added, 'I shouldn't really talk like that. You won't tell him, will you?'

'No, of course not.'

The mention of the motorbike reminded Onion about Mrs Toadstool. 'Here,' he said. 'Where's Mrs

Toa– Mrs Tunstall? I didn't see her in the living room.'

'She's in her room, lying down,' Danilo replied. 'Always needs her nap in the afternoon. She dozes right off in the chair if she doesn't remember to go to bed, the sleepy-head. Come on, now, move along before I get shouted at.'

Onion started back down the hall, glancing behind just once as he went, and felt a shiver run through him. He could swear Alexander's one good eye was staring straight at him.

CHAPTER SIX:
—
THE CHEAPSKATE

Granny had been busy. Enlisting the help of the staff, she'd organised pots of tea, her buns and some biscuits for everyone and had the first volunteers up and learning the basic steps of a waltz.

'Now, follow my count, aaaaand ... *one*, two, three, *one*, two, three ... don't slump, Joe, dear. Back straight, head up, that's it.' She showed him the proper stance. 'There you are – now try not to step on Sive's feet ... and *one*, two, three and ... Lovely form there, Máire, but you should be like you're stepping round the corners of a box ... step and step and step ... settle down, you're not dancing a jig, love. And together, everyone ... *one*, two, three, *one*, two, three … Onion, dear, it's not the slow dance at the end of the disco. You don't have to wrap your arms around your partner.'

The other Five O's laughed, but it was no joke for Onion. His partner, Ursula Stockton, was a stocky lady who took heavy breaths and heavy steps and wasn't very steady on her feet. She kept leaning on him, so that he ended up half-buried in her ample bosom as she dug her elbows into his shoulders. Still, she was enjoying herself, and he thought that was no bad thing – these folks looked like they needed a bit of fun in their lives.

Ursula finally ran out of breath and Onion was able to take a break, as nobody else was waiting for a turn. Dallan and Sive were coping well with their partners, and Clíona was with Eoin, the man in the motorised wheelchair. He kept rolling over her toes, so she had to try and do the steps around him while keeping her feet as far back as possible, which gave her a somewhat diagonal appearance.

Onion was thirsty, and he didn't want tea or coffee, so he headed to the kitchen to ask for a glass of water. He stopped at the half-open door because Leary was in there, giving orders to the two members of staff with him.

'Don't throw out those used teabags,' he was saying. 'You can still squeeze another round of tea out of those. *Two* rounds. And when that O'Brien woman goes, make sure you turn off the heating again. We're not made of money.'

CHAPTER SIX: THE CHEAPSKATE

'And take in any of the leftover buns before those old farts can gobble them all down. Stockton definitely had more than two and O'Halloran took a bun, a Bourbon Cream *and* a Jammie Dodger, the pig. Who said you could give out the biscuits? They'll be getting notions, that lot, if they're pampered like that. Do you want them to think they'll get biscuits every time there's visitors – is that what you want?'

Top 5 Ways Austin Leary Is a Complete Cheapskate

1. Reusing teabags

2. Turning the bedsheets around instead of cleaning them

3. Watering down the milk, soup and even bottled water with tap water

4. Handing out big old jumpers instead of putting the heating on

5. Serving cream crackers and cheese spread for dinner three days a week

'Oh, and I notice *Alexander* is out of his room again,' Leary went on. 'I've told you before to keep him in his room – *especially* when there's visitors.'

'We didn't move him,' Onion heard Danilo reply. 'That kid found him out there, but nobody moved him.'

'Spare me your excuses!' Leary snapped. 'You expect me to believe he wheeled himself down the hall? Inconceivable! If I've told you once, I've told you a thousand times, he's not for public viewing. *I'm* the only one who talks to him. *I'm* the only one he sees. Is that understood? And while we're talking about wheelchairs, Eoin's wheelchair battery is only to be charged every second day – where does he need to go anyway? The electricity bills in this place are ridiculous, especially since the power keeps going. I mean, what am I paying for, eh? Imagine paying bills for electricity that keeps failing. It's a crime what they charge for electricity these days ...'

Onion decided he wasn't that desperate for a drink of water. He went back out to the living room. Granny was trying to show Francie how to do the waltz. Sive was showing Ursula some hip-hop dance steps while they waited for Granny. Dallan was talking to Eoin, the guy in the wheelchair, about art. Though Dallan didn't know much about art, he was a master of the art of waffling on any subject. Clíona was fiddling with the rubbish television, partly to improve the reception and partly to experience what life would have been like in a previous century.

Onion was standing by the door that led through to the kitchen when saw something out of the corner of his wonky eye and nearly jumped out of his skin: Alexander was sitting there in his wheelchair. The man was as deathly still as before, yet he seemed to have appeared out of nowhere. He looked like he was watching Clíona. Onion took a suck on his inhaler and looked down at the man. 'How did you do that?' he whispered.

The man gave no sign of answering, but when Onion glanced away and then back again, he found Alexander's good eye staring up at him. Onion's wonky eye went on the move again, as if his eye and Alexander's were trying to communicate.

Clíona saw them and came over, her notebook in her hand again, and it reminded Onion about the notebook stuck down the side of Alex's chair. Did the man have anything going on in that head of his, or was Danilo right that there wasn't much left upstairs? And if that was so, what did he need a notebook for?

'Who's this?' Clíona asked. She leaned in closer to the man. 'Hello, there. I'm Clíona.'

'His name's Alexander Yuryev,' Onion replied. 'He's Russian. That's a cool scar, isn't it? Nobody knows how he got it. It's like someone stuck a lightsabre in his face.'

'Yeah ...' Clíona said, and from the way she said it, and the look on her face, Onion knew that wheels had started turning in her head. Clíona had a lot of wheels in her head. 'Are you a science fiction fan, Alexander? I *love* science fiction.'

'INCONCEIVABLE!' a voice from behind them exclaimed. It was Leary again. 'Who left *him* here? Danilo? *Danilo!* For the last time, take Alexander back to his room! And lock the door if you have to. Nobody goes in and nobody comes out – do you understand?'

Danilo came through, mumbling an apology, and was about to wheel the Russian man away when Leary stopped him for a second and reached down to Alexander's lap, pulling out the notebook.

Scowling, he caught the children looking at him and a flush of guilt crossed his face.

'My notebook,' he said, clearing his throat. 'I wondered where that had got to.'

He went to put it in his trouser pocket, but it slipped and dropped to the floor, flopping open on a random page. Onion immediately bent down to pick it up, but Clíona beat him to it. The pages were filled with mathematical symbols he couldn't understand.

'Oh, Maxwell's equations!' Clíona said, handing the notebook back. 'Are you a physicist, Mr Leary?'

'I dabble a bit. Thank you,' Leary grunted. 'Isn't nearly time for you to be going?'

'It is, I'm afraid!' Granny said in a chirpy voice. 'But don't you worry, we'll all be back tomorrow, God willing! And we can come earlier, so we'll have even more time for dance practice!'

Leary tried not to groan too loudly. And so did the Five O's.

CHAPTER SEVEN:
FAMILY BLOOD

Walking down the driveway of St Brigit's of the Weeping Wound, they emerged from the gate to find the black van with tinted windows parked across the road – the van that had caught Mrs Toadstool while she'd been doing wheelies on the motorbike. At least two men were in the van, and a woman was leaning against the front of it. The same woman in the black suit who had winked at them after Mrs Toadstool had disappeared into the back of the van. She lowered her sunglasses slightly to eye the Five O's as they came out.

Then she smiled slightly and arched an eyebrow.

'There's something scary about that woman,' Onion said.

'Oh, ya think?' Sive snorted. 'She looks like the business manager for a team of assassins.' The other three nodded in agreement.

Granny didn't hear the comment because she was absorbed in reading something on a piece of paper she was holding. 'Onion, I need you to go and get a few things in the shopping centre,' she said. 'You need to get there before the chemist's closes. Some of the folk in the home were running short of some things, and that Leary fellow doesn't keep them well supplied. Between you and me, I think he might be a bit cheap.'

Oh, ya think? Onion nearly said, but didn't.

'Here, I've got a list for you,' Granny went on. 'Make sure you go to the chemist's first. Don't worry if you don't know what these things are – the staff will have it all there. Here's the money.'

Onion reluctantly took the list and the money and looked to his friends for support. Clíona was off in the clouds, thinking about who knew what. Dallan was turned away, whistling and making a bad show of pretending to be distracted by something.

'Come on.' Sive sighed, popping a new stick of gum in her mouth. 'I'll go with you.'

Onion gave her a grateful smile, and they set off up the road towards the shopping centre while Granny and the others waited for the bus home. It was only a ten-minute walk, and Onion was half-hoping the pharmacy would be closed when he got there. The place made him nervous.

On the way in, they saw a couple of guys high up on a cherry-picker, using the machine to move back and forth so they could work on the big illuminated sign over the door. Onion craned his neck to look upwards. As he did so, he spotted a black helicopter high in the sky above them. The two men in the cherry-picker looked up too, as the helicopter came in lower and swept past, making very little noise, almost as if its engine had been silenced somehow.

'I know what you're thinking,' Sive said. 'But there's nothing mysterious about that. It's just a ... y'know ... a helicopter.'

Onion thought she sounded like she was trying to convince herself.

The walk didn't take long enough, so the chemist's was still open. Onion and Sive hung around in the shopping centre's small mall, still reluctant to go in. The mall was an old place, with just a supermarket and a small row of shops down one side. Onion felt his heart sink as he saw Derek and his mates sitting on a bench together, all of them staring at their phones. So far, they hadn't noticed the two younger kids.

'What's up, losers?'

CHAPTER SEVEN: FAMILY BLOOD

Onion and Sive looked at each other in dismay, then turned to find Tina Dalton standing behind them. As usual, she had her two henchmen flanking her, Barry and Larry Bang, collectively known as the Bang-Off-Them Brothers, though nobody called them that to their faces. If Derek was obsessed with smothering his body odour in chemical odour, the brothers had no such concerns. And unlike Derek, they needed all the help they could get. They were as smelly as they were big, and for kids their age, they were *huge*. Their menacing facial features were as blunt and dull as their minds.

Tina, on the other hand, had a mind like a surgeon's scalpel and smelled of lavender and world domination. She was beautiful, with blonde ringlets framing delicate bone structure, full red lips, a touch of charming freckles and big blue eyes that could see fear in a human heart. Half the kids in Ballinlud's primary schools were scared of her, and that was only because the rest of them hadn't met her yet. She had a knack for choosing just the right type of cruelty for whichever victim came before her. Even secondary school kids like Derek treated her with a wary respect. The Bang-Off-Them Brothers worshipped her like a goddess.

Tina snatched the paper out of Onion's hand and cast her eyes down the list. 'Doing a bit of shopping, O'Brien? What have we got here?'

Onion didn't answer, partly out of fear and partly because he couldn't tell her. He didn't know what half of the words meant.

'It's none of your business,' Sive said, reaching out. 'Give that back, it's not yours!'

Larry Bang caught Sive's arm before it could touch his goddess's sleeve. 'Hands off, Deafness, or I'll spread that nose across your face.'

Sive yanked her arm away. She wasn't deaf, but she did wear hearing aids, and though Larry's insult didn't bother her, his warning did. She knew Larry would happily thump a girl in the face to show Tina what a big man he was. And if he got started, his brother would join in. And Onion would be little help in a fight against those two.

'Ha!' Tina cackled. 'Having a few problems, are we, O'Brien?'

'What do you mean?' Onion asked defensively.

'"Wig tape",' Tina said, grinning. 'Helps keep your wig stuck down. Having trouble keeping your hair on, are you? Oh, and *perfume*. Oooh, I never figured you for the type. Bit *out of date*, that scent, but the oul' ones love it. And look at this. These are tablets for cleaning false teeth. You have to soak them overnight. You do have some **dark secrets!'**

The Bang brothers sniggered their low, coughing laughs.

'Those aren't for me ...' Onion was trying to say.

'And wait!' Tina cried. 'This is stuff for an *itchy bum!* Got an *itchy bum* too, O'Brien? A wig, old lady's perfume, false teeth *and* an itchy bum. You're a bit of a mess, aren't you, eh? You should take better care of yourself!'

The brothers laughed again. Their goddess was hilarious.

'Those are for different people!' Onion protested. 'This isn't funny, give that back! *Give it back!*'

He was getting upset now, and not just because of her teasing, but because she was teasing the people back at the home, and that wasn't fair. They were *old*. They couldn't help being old. Stuff just happened to you after you'd been hanging around the world for that long. It was like she was mocking his granny or grandad, or *anyone's* granny or grandad, and that wasn't on. You didn't mock grandparents.

'Hang on,' Sive said, her eyes narrowing at Tina and her gum-chewing paused for a moment.

'How do *you* know what those things are?'

Tina's face went stiff, offended that anyone should question her, then she waved dismissively and sniffed. 'My uncle Austin runs the old folks' home down the road. Dunno why – he *hates* old people. He's always moaning about their problems. He goes on about this kind of stuff to my dad all the time.'

Onion and Sive exchanged looks. It came as no surprise at all that Austin Leary was Tina Dalton's uncle. Nastiness ran through her family blood.

'... But he makes money out of the old farts for doing next to nothing,' she went on, 'and that's all he cares about. He's almost as big a loser as you lot. Now ... how much is this shopping list worth to you?'

'What?' Onion said, his face dropping. 'We're not paying you anything. Give it back!'

'Barry, *eat the list.*' Tina handed it back to her henchman, who took the piece of paper.

He went to put it in his mouth and Onion dived forward to stop him. Unfortunately, he knocked

Tina over as he did so, and though he managed to seize the list from Barry's hand, he looked down and a shiver ran through him as he saw Tina sprawled on her back on the floor.

'Oh-my-God-I'm-so-sorry,' Onion squeaked.

Barry and Larry clamped onto Onion and Sive with their meaty fists. Tina's eyes fixed on Onion, cold and unblinking. She rose up slowly, in one smooth motion, like something from a Japanese horror movie. Her arm raised up, dead straight, and she said in a quiet, rasping voice, 'END THEM!'

'Oh, jaypers ...' Sive muttered.

'There a problem here?'

Onion heard the words and, somewhere between terror and relief, he managed not to pee himself. Even before he looked around Barry's oversized shoulder, the tell-tale over-applied musk of Lynx Africa hit him like an eye-watering fog. It was Derek and four of his mates, teenage lads who were as tall as the Bang-Off-Them Brothers, if not quite so wide. Derek was happy to thump Onion whenever the mood took him, but that was a big brother's privilege. He wasn't about to let the local bully and her goons take liberties. There were principles to observe.

Tina did some quick manpower calculations in her head and decided this wasn't the time for a fight. It didn't matter – she had all the time in the world. She knew where Onion O'Brien lived. And now Derek was on her list too.

'No problem,' she said, with an icy calm and a smile that would have made Dracula shudder. 'No problem at all. I'll see you around, Onion. Sometime soon, *I'll be seeing you.*'

Onion gulped and tried to stop his wonky eye from waggling wildly. Everyone knew Tina Dalton kept her promises.

CHAPTER EIGHT: — KNOWN TO THE GARDAÍ

Onion didn't sleep much that night. It didn't help that the air in their room had been replaced by Derek's pungent deodorant, and it filled his nose long after he fell asleep, so he was brought back to that moment in his dreams, over and over again, where he was staring into Tina Dalton's eyes as if she was some giant constrictor snake that was going to crush the breath out of him and swallow him whole.

Onion woke from a nightmare about suffocating to find Derek farting in his face, and he sat up, coughing and gasping for breath. His brother was already dressed, brushed and deodorised.

'Granny wants us both up,' Derek growled, checking his hair in the mirror on the wardrobe door. 'Up you get, sunshine. If I don't get to lie in, then neither do you.'

It was Sunday morning. They had to go to Mass. Granny never missed Mass, and she made sure her grandkids didn't either. Grandad, somehow, managed to have something else more urgent to do most Sundays. Groaning and rubbing his eyes, Onion put on his glasses and eye patch, took a breath of his inhaler and pulled his good clothes out of the wardrobe.

He'd told Derek about the strange goings-on at St Brigit's of the Weeping Wound, hoping to recruit his big brother in the investigation, but Derek had told him to cop himself on and stop being an eejit. It was an old folks' home; there was nothing going on. Nothing happened in these places – that was the whole point of them. It was where you went to chill out and watch telly for the last years of your life.

Derek's ideal life would involve chilling and watching telly all day, or being on his phone, so he couldn't imagine why anyone would do anything else once they'd retired.

'There *is* something going on,' Onion insisted quietly. 'You don't know anything. But I'll prove it.'

'You will in my bum,' Derek said. 'Now hurry up. If we're late for Mass again, Granny'll eat the heads off us.'

Most of the people at Mass that morning were getting on in years, and it occurred to Onion that he'd probably do more praying, too, if he was their age. Elderly people had a lot to deal with. He also noticed that Tina was there with her family. They always put on a real show of being respectable, even though most of them were villains of one sort or another. She smiled across the aisle at him in a way that made her look like a blessed saint to anyone else, but turned his blood to water.

'See you soon, Onion!' she said to him, as they left the church.

Onion's dread dragged on him as he walked out into the car park. He saw Derek had a furious face on him, though he was careful not to let Granny see how he was feeling.

'I have to go to that bleedin' old folks' home with you today,' he muttered through gritted teeth. 'Because none of you flippin' losers can *dance*. I can't believe it!'

When he was Onion's age, Granny had paid Derek to help out at some dance classes she'd held in the church hall to raise money for the church. Derek had enjoyed it more than he liked to admit, and it turned out he showed promise as a ballroom dancer. Given that he lived in the desperately ordinary suburb of Ballinlud, there was nothing he could do with this skill, and he didn't want to spend his teenage years dancing with people four times his age, so he'd given it up as soon as he could. But Granny had not forgotten, and she told him his time had come to shine again.

'I can't believe it!' he said again. 'I was going to the shopping centre and now I have to waste the day doin' bleedin' waltzes and foxtrots! You're all useless, the lot of yiz! And if you tell any of my mates I'm doing this, I'll replace your face with your bum cheeks!'

'OK, promise, but this is great,' Onion said. 'You can help us figure out what's going on up there. It'll be the full Five O's team back together again.'

'How many times do I have to say it? There's *nothing* going on and *I'm not in your stupid gang*!'

So it was an enlarged group that arrived at the gate of St Brigit's of the Weeping Wound early that afternoon, with Onion, Derek and Sive still dressed in their Sunday best, Dallan dressed in good clothes because he *always* dressed in good clothes, and Clíona dressed in her usual oversized shirt, T-shirt and combats because the only time she didn't was when she had to wear her school uniform.

As they walked up the driveway, they saw the light in the building's dull reception flicker and go off. They heard what sounded like a crackle from the power lines that ran along the road.

'Another power cut,' Granny said, tutting. 'That's no good. I don't have any batteries for the stereo. Derek, we might have to use your phone.'

'Those folks are too old, Granny,' Derek said. 'This kind of technology would blow their minds.'

'Don't be ridiculous,' she replied. 'Music is music, dear. It doesn't matter what kind of box it's coming out of.'

Derek's shocked expression suggested the nature of the box mattered *way* more than Granny seemed to think. He was distracted from pointing this out, however, when a garda car pulled past them and parked in the space beside Austin Leary's motorbike. The man and woman who got out looked at the bike, then at each other and then strode up to the front door.

It was Garda Fergus Plunkett and Garda Bridie Judge again. Granny motioned for the Five O's to wait, holding far enough back that they didn't embarrass Mr Leary but close enough that Granny could hear what was being said. She knew good gossip material when she saw it.

The CEO of St Brigit's of the Weeping Wound was summoned outside and the Ferg gestured towards the motorbike. 'Is this your motorcycle, sir?'

'Yes, it is,' Leary answered testily. 'What about it?'

'Sir, this motorcycle was involved in an incident that occurred in this vicinity yesterday afternoon,' the Ferg said, in his best garda voice. 'It involved a lady of advanced years who was motorcycling in a highly irresponsible manner, resulting in a high-speed pursuit with a garda vehicle, driven by Garda Judge here and accompanied by me, that was called out in response to said incident. Were you, Mr Leary, aware of this woman's activities?'

'I don't know what you're talking about,' Leary replied. 'This bike didn't leave this driveway from the time I got to work to the time I left at five o'clock. Nobody was riding it anywhere – and especially not a *woman*. No one rides this baby but me. You clearly have it mistaken for someone else's.'

'It was the same bike. It was the same licence plate,' Garda Judge said in a much simpler, sterner garda voice. The Ferg talked the talk, but Judge walked the walk. 'Mr Leary, are you saying you weren't aware that it was being used?'

'Nobody was using my bike,' Leary stated firmly. 'Especially not a *woman*.'

'Yes, they were! We saw her!' Onion shouted – he couldn't help himself blurting out at moments like this, much to his friends' constant dismay. 'It was Mrs Toa– Mrs Tat– eh, Mrs Tunstall! We all saw her yesterday. She was doing wheelies and everything. It was awesome!'

The two guards swivelled to look back at Granny and her gang of kids. The Ferg wrinkled his nose. Judge raised an eyebrow.

'Why can't you ever keep your mouth shut?' Derek whispered.

'He's right,' Dallan spoke up, obviously wanting to stir things a bit more. 'We saw Mrs Tunstall riding that bike yesterday. Did she steal it, Mr Leary? Is that what happened?'

'*Tunstall?* That sleepy old bat?' Leary exclaimed. Then he seemed to think about it for a moment and it looked like something troubling occurred to him. He clearly wasn't comfortable talking to the guards. 'I suppose ... I suppose that must be what happened. No doubt it was her *medication*. It can make her a bit delirious. That must be it. She just lost the run of herself, the poor dear.'

'We'll need to interview her, sir, if you don't mind,' the Ferg said, 'to ascertain her whereabouts during the incident and assess if her future motorcycling activities are likely to be a further threat to the public.'

It was then that a dark figure swept past the Five O's. It was the woman in the black suit, who seemed to have come from nowhere, moving swiftly despite the fact that her legs didn't seem to be in any rush.

'Perhaps I can be of assistance?' she said. Her Irish American voice had a tone that implied the 'assistance' she was offering would be of a supervisory nature, in that she was about to tell everyone what to do and they would have little choice but to do it. 'I'm Elektra McGaffney, the new proprietor of this facility.'

'The – what?' Leary stammered. 'You're the new owner? Since when?'

'Since my organisation bought it yesterday,' she replied, holding up a legal-looking document.

'And which organisation is that?' Garda Judge asked.

'The organisation that just *phoned your boss*,' McGaffney replied.

The two women were standing a metre apart, each one measuring up the other. Each one looked smart and hard as nails and unwilling to take any nonsense. Judge was about to say something, when her phone rang. She pulled it from her pocket. 'Garda Judge … Yes?' She listened for a moment. A frown appeared on her face and she glanced at her partner. 'But, sir – no, sir – I don't think that – yes, sir. Yes, understood. Without any further delay.'

She ended the call and put the phone back in her pocket. She stared at Elektra McGaffney for a moment. 'We've been called back to the station, Fergus,' she told her partner. 'And there's to be no more "interference" in Ms McGaffney's work.' Then she said to the other woman, 'You've got my attention now, McGaffney. You've made me curious. You may be able to pull strings, but I can follow those strings to find out where they lead.'

'Oh, please do,' McGaffney said, with a slight smile. 'Nothing gives me greater pleasure than watching a mouse run through one of those little mazes. Now, if you'll excuse me, shuffle on, Garda. I've got work to do.'

And with that, the two guards left. And Elektra McGaffney turned her attention to Granny and the Five O's.

CHAPTER NINE:
—
THE BLACK SUITS

McGaffney stared at the mixed group in front of her. 'And you are?'

'We're here to teach a dance class, ma'am,' Granny said. 'The children got up to some mischief here yesterday – you know, acting the maggot, if you will' – trying to be posh again with her *if you will* – 'and we're making amends by facilitating a dance class for the stimulation of the minds and promotion of the health of the residents.' Granny now went into full-on posh with her *facilitating*, *stimulation* and *promotion*, words she only knew because Grandad loved shouting at his crossword clues in the paper.

CHAPTER NINE: THE BLACK SUITS

Elektra McGaffney inspired caution. Anyone who could make the guards go away with a phone call was someone to be respected ... and perhaps feared. She had the eyes of a wolf and the voice of a teacher. You didn't mess with that voice.

'Very well,' McGaffney said, waving them away. 'Continue. Mr Leary, a word in your office, please.'

Leary looked in shock, like some cartoon character who'd run off a cliff and had only just realised he was hanging out over a long, long drop. He turned obediently and shuffled into reception and through to his office. McGaffney followed him in and closed the door. The power was back on, and the sad light was doing its best to illuminate the little hallway. Like the rest of the building, though, it was too faded and cheap to brighten anyone's day.

Derek was still sulking as Granny led them into the living room and began setting up for the dance class, but Onion could tell his brother was curious now too. There could be no doubt about it any more: something weird was definitely going down in St Brigit's of the Weeping Wound. Onion kept trying to catch his eye, hoping to get him talking as they danced, but Derek was having none of it. He wasn't ready to believe just yet.

Sive was having a chat, comparing different kinds of hearing aids with one of the women, and in the process was trying to draw information out of her about life in the nursing home. Dallan was less shy about his curiosity. As soon as he got a break from the dancing, he slipped out into reception to listen at the door to Leary's office. Onion was dying to join him; instead, he was with Ursula Stockton again, and she was being a lot more energetic today. He noticed, too, that she had the number 2 written on her arm in black marker.

Just like Mrs Toadstool and the number 5, when he'd watched her go past on the motorbike.

Granny saw that Onion was struggling to stay ahead of the large-figured lady, and she told Derek to take over. Ursula was very happy with the exchange, and Derek showed her some more steps she could work into the routine she was learning. She picked them up immediately. It turned out Ursula had been quite the athlete in her day, and she was in a chatty mood. Derek thought she was also a bit full of herself, because to hear her talk, she'd been champion of *everything* at one point or another.

Top 5 Things Ursula Stockton Was Champion of, Back in the Day

1. Karate – signature move: the spinning kick

2. Pole vault – signature move: the double-leg drop

3. Wrestling – signature move: the powerbomb

4. Breakdancing– signature move: the head-slide

5. Cake decoration – signature move: the buttercream flower

'Can't we have something with a bit more *oomph* in it?' Ursula said as the tune ended. She opened the tape deck, took out the tape and changed it for one she had in her pocket. Giving Granny a naughty look, she said, **'LET'S LIFT THE ROOF OFF THIS PLACE!'**

'Uh-oh,' Onion said, as he saw Sive come to the same realisation and hurriedly step off the dance floor. Together, they hauled Clíona off to the side too.

The opening lines of Gloria Gaynor's disco classic 'I Will Survive' came bursting out of the speakers. Several of the elderly women screamed in delight and threw their handbags into the middle of the floor.

'Eh, what's goin' on now?' Derek asked, looking around him.

And then, with a whip of her hand, Ursula sent him spinning across the dance floor, just catching his hand and pulling him to her as Gloria sang about how her man had done her wrong. And it only got wilder from there.

CHAPTER NINE: THE BLACK SUITS

Most of the other ladies could only sway and clap, leaving Ursula to do her moves, switching between the Hustle, the Boogaloo, the Cha-Cha … fast and frantic, with Derek struggling to keep up. And yet … he was enjoying it. Onion could see the wonder on his brother's face, hypnotised by Ursula's dazzling power and grace. He was *loving* it. And still trying not to show it.

Danilo and some of the other carers were clapping in time to the music and whooping encouragement. Ursula was losing the run of herself, kicking chairs aside to make more room, swinging free of Derek to jump up onto a table. Danilo gasped in alarm, and went to call her back down, but from there, she leaped into Derek's arms …

A move that Derek was completely

unprepared for. He caught her, staggered backwards, toppled through into the dining room and fell flat on his back, hurling Ursula over his head and through the half-open kitchen door. There came the almighty crash of plates and cutlery and then Ursula's cackling laughter as she slumped back against a fallen food trolley, heaving in hysterics.

Most of the old folk were giggling too. Granny, however, was mortified, not knowing what to make of this at all. Ursula was calming down and now she was looking nervous. She shook her head and blinked, as if something important had just occurred to her. Then she looked at the number on her wrist and bit her lip.

Onion stepped past Derek and held his hand out to her. 'Mrs Stockton? Is everything OK? I think we should …'

He wasn't sure what they should do, and it didn't matter. Ursula scrambled to her feet, slipping on loose cutlery and broken crockery. Then she pushed through another door that led out into a hallway and made a quick exit. Onion rushed after her, wanting to check that she was all right. When he made it out of the hallway, she was gone.

Checking behind him to see if anyone was watching, he carried on down the hall. This was another section of the building with bedrooms, and there were names on all the doors. Ursula's was here, though the door was open and she wasn't in her room. She must have gone into someone else's. Further down, Onion found a room marked 'Alexander Yuryev'. The door was locked. Hadn't Leary said that the Russian wasn't allowed out of his room? But why bother locking it when Alexander couldn't move on his own?

He came to the back door, which led out into the garden, though there was no sign of her out there. Facing the back door across the hall was the door to a utility room. Onion opened it to find shelves of bed linen, a mop and bucket, a stack of hot-water bottles, some crutches and other odds and ends. There was nothing special about the place … except that Alexander's wheelchair was there, folded up and tucked in under the shelves. Onion was sure it was the same one. He wondered why it wasn't just kept in his room. It wasn't like the old guy needed space to wander round.

Coming back out, he shut the door just before two of McGaffney's black-suited goons stepped out of the kitchen into the hallway. Ignoring Onion, they put a case on the floor, opened it and took out a small surveillance camera. With a few practised movements, they screwed it into the wall above the kitchen door. With a remote control, they tested that it could swivel left and right. Then they each took another camera from the case and strode to either end of the hallway, one of them passing Onion, and attached the cameras to the walls at each end.

Onion walked back to the kitchen. Passing the case, he could see its contents: more cameras and other gadgets he couldn't recognise. This was all getting very weird.

CHAPTER NINE: THE BLACK SUITS

'Your granny's leaving,' one of the men said, a big blocky guy with chestnut brown skin and a chiselled face. His eyes were hidden by sunglasses, which he was wearing indoors on a dull, cloudy day. 'You'd best be running along. Maybe you could come back tomorrow.' He pointed at the camera over the door, with a slight smile. 'See you then, eh?'

CHAPTER TEN: — CONSPIRACY THEORIES

Dallan looked from one face to another as the Five O's sat in Onion and Derek's small bedroom.

'It's aliens,' he said. 'Everyone knows that the Men in Black control alien activity on Earth. It's the most famous secret in the world. They're here because there are aliens here.'

'*People* in Black,' Sive corrected him. '*Men* in Black is sexist. Some of them are women. Their *leader* is a woman, so they're *People* in Black.'

'It's highly unlikely that there are aliens in Ballinlud,' Clíona said.

'No, it's rubbish,' Derek stated firmly. 'This is not about aliens.'

Derek was there against his better judgement. He generally considered anything the Five O's did as childish, sad or stupid or all three, and yet even he couldn't resist wondering what was going on at St Brigit's of the Weeping Wound. For the moment, he was willing to put up with these saddos until he got some answers, even if they did annoy the bejaypers out of him.

Top 5 Things That Annoy Derek about the Five O's

1. The fact that there are only four of them

2. They keep insisting that Derek is in their stupid gang

3. They go along with Onion's stupid adventures

4. They keep distracting him from his phone

5. None of them smell of Lynx Africa

Derek was still reeling from his dancing experience with Ursula, and though he hated to admit it to himself, that dance had awoken a passion in him that had slumbered for too long. He was already feeling the need to go out to some club and bust a groove, as the oul' ones said.

'It is *not* about aliens,' he grunted again.

'But that's what the Men in Black do,' Dallan insisted.

'*People* in Black,' Sive repeated.

'All right, *People* in Black,' Dallan said, shrugging. 'That's what they do. They control alien activity. And the aliens are doing experiments on the old folk.'

'But they might not be the Men – eh, People in Black,' Onion said. 'They might just be people, y'know … all dressed in black suits. Even the women.'

Derek was sitting on the only chair, at the small desk behind the door. The others were sitting on the beds, trying not to comment on the ever-present odour of Lynx Africa. There was a loud droning from Molly's room across the landing, where she was playing with the hoover. Onion had taken it out of the cupboard for her to keep her busy and stop her from disturbing them. Molly had been delighted.

'Maybe it's a retirement home for spies,' Sive suggested. 'And they've all got … like … super skills that are supposed to be kept secret, and McGaffney's here because Leary hasn't been keeping a lid on the place.'

'Granny has known Mrs Toadstool all her life,' Derek pointed out. 'She'd know if old Tattle was a spy.'

'Would she?' Sive asked. 'That's the whole point of being a spy, isn't it? That nobody knows you're a spy.'

'Unless you're James Bond,' Onion said. 'Everyone knows he's a spy. He's, like, the least secret spy there's ever been.'

'He's not a real spy,' Sive said. 'That's just pretend. These are *real* secret agents, so nobody knows what they are. Except for the People in Black, who are ... whatchamacallits ... eh ...'

'Enforcers?' Clíona said.

'Yeah, enforcers. They're here to keep things quiet.'

'I think it might be *mutants*,' Clíona said, and everyone turned to her. She was the smartest one in the group, at least when it came to science and stuff, so any theory she had was worth listening to. 'The way these old people are showing skills that nobody knew they had? Or – or skills that maybe they had when they were young, and now they're showing up again?

CHAPTER TEN: CONSPIRACY THEORIES

'What if everyone in that home was a subject of some secret experiment when they were young that mutated their genes, and now they're getting old and dotty, they've got to be monitored by the government in case their powers get out of control? Maybe that's why they have numbers on their wrists – that was each person's number in the experiment.'

'That could be it,' Onion said.

'No, I think it's spies,' Sive said.

'Aliens,' Dallan insisted. 'Or ... or ... or maybe they were trained as spies because of the experiments that were done on them by aliens when they were young.'

'You're all bleedin' space cadets,' Derek growled. 'This could all be some big prank for some show on the telly. It's a *set-up*, I'm tellin' yiz. Someone's out there laughing their heads off at us. It'll all be on YouTube next week. *You've Been Old-Peopled* it'll be called.

'So how did Ursula dance like that?' Onion asked. 'How did Francie O'Halloran beat Grandad at darts when he can hardly see and his hands shake like fish? How did Mrs Toadstool do a wheelie on a motorbike?'

'I don't know, I'm just sayin' ...' Derek pretended to play with his fringe, not wanting to meet his brother's eyes. 'They've probably got stuntmen dressed up or something ...'

There was silence as they all pondered the situation.

'I think I've seen Alexander's face before,' Clíona said after a while. 'I could swear I have, but I can't remember where. It was something to do with what happened to his face. I've already looked him up online, but I didn't find anything.'

'Granny wants us to go back tomorrow. I think she's curious too,' Onion told them.

'I'm cringin' at the thought of it!' Derek groaned, shaking his head. 'Everyone's going to hear about that dance!'

Their grandmother was still on the phone downstairs, talking to her friends. The strange goings-on at the nursing home made for prime gossip, and when it came to spreading news, Instagram or Twitter had nothing on the oul' granny network.

'Can't believe we didn't get that dance on video,' Sive chuckled.

'Shut up, you!' Derek snapped. 'And remember, if any of you tell my mates –'

'You'll put our bum cheeks on our face or something like that,' interrupted Sive.

Even though it was daylight, they had the light on in the room, as the window was small and it was always a bit dull in there. The light flickered and went out. They heard the hoover cut out too and Molly uttered a loud moan. Sive, who was nearest the light switch, got up and tried it, though they all knew it wouldn't work even before she clicked it a couple of times. She opened the door and they could still hear Granny downstairs on the phone, but the phone ran on a different system.

'Granny!' Molly opened her bedroom door and called out, 'The electric's gone off again! The

hoover's not working!'

'It'll be back on in a while, love!' Granny shouted back up the stairs. 'Why don't you come down here and paint my toenails? You can go back to your hoovering later.'

Dallan remembered something then and pulled a folded piece of paper from his back pocket. 'Here, I never showed yiz this! Eoin did it.'

Unfolding it, he held up it for them to see. It was a cartoon drawing, a pretty good one, of Derek and Ursula dancing. Eoin, the guy in the motorised wheelchair, must have drawn it pretty fast, considering the whole dance had only lasted a few minutes. Onion was there in the background, and Sive and Clíona, as well as a couple of the residents. Mrs Toadstool, Pixel Pat and Alexander were there too, though he hadn't been in the room at the time. The pencil lines were simple, but they caught the likenesses of the faces with real skill.

'Wonder why he drew Alexander in?' Sive said.

'I wonder why he drew Alexander *smiling*?' Onion added.

It was true. The man who apparently had nothing left upstairs was sitting upright in his wheelchair, looking alert, a gentle smile distorting the scar on his cheek. And then Onion noticed something else. Alexander was holding a notebook to his chest, as if he was protecting it.

And there was a number 12 written on the back of his wrist.

CHAPTER ELEVEN: GRANDAD FACES INTERROGATION

The hoover started up again in Molly's room and the light in the boys' bedroom flickered on. The power was back. Seconds later, the doorbell rang. On reflex, Onion stood up and looked out the window to see who it was. He immediately ducked down, his wonky eye wide with fear.

'IT'S THEM!' he whimpered.

The others rushed to the window. Sure enough, a black SUV was parked at the kerb beyond the gate, and a man and a woman in black suits were standing facing the front door. She was tall, blonde and skinny; he was short, dark and built like the cab of a truck. They both wore sunglasses.

'Paddy, can you get that?' Onion heard his granny say downstairs. 'Molly's doing my toes.'

Grandad muttered a few swear words and something about what was the world coming to when a man couldn't enjoy his newspaper in peace on a Sunday afternoon without having to answer the bleedin' door. Then he trudged out into the hall to open said door. Derek cracked open the bedroom door a few centimetres so they could all hear better.

'Sir, are you Patrick O'Brien, the owner of this residence?' the woman asked.

'Who's asking?' Grandad replied.

'And are you the guardian of … eh, *Onion* and Derek O'Brien?'

'I'm still waiting for you to tell me who you are,' Grandad said in a sterner voice. 'Bloody young people, you never introduce yourselves any more.'

'Sir, we're with the government, working with the intelligence services –'

'Intelligence? In the government?' Grandad interrupted with a loud sniff. 'When did that start? I've been waiting my whole life for some sign of intelligence from the government.'

Top 5 Things Grandad Hates about the Government

1. No respect for the workers

2. He'd do the whole politics thing himself, if he wasn't busy doing a proper job. Sure, any eejit could do it

3. Only an eejit would get into politics, so all politicians are eejits

4. It's the smart ones you've got to look out for. They'd take the shirt off your back, given half a chance. Con artists, the lot o' them

5. They've got hooves for feet

'Sir, if you'd just answer a few of our –' the woman in black tried again.

'You still haven't shown me any identification, yeh chancer. Who in the name of God are ye? You could be anybody! "Hello, pleased to meet you. I'm a stranger knocking on your door looking for your bank details so I can steal your house!"'

This interview clearly wasn't going the way the agents had expected. There was a rustle of clothing as they produced identification cards, and then a pause as Grandad looked at them.

'"Agency for Really Strange Emergencies"?' Grandad read out loud, barking a laugh. **'A-R-S-E?** You work for ARSE?'

'We call it "A-FoRSE",' the man said in a tetchy voice.

'Never heard of it. Sounds made up. And what interest does ARSE have in my grandsons?' Grandad giggled.

'It's *A-FoRSE*. And we just have some questions regarding their connection to St Brigit's of the Weeping Wound.'

'What's that?'

'The … the *nursing home*, sir.' The woman sighed. 'Where your wife and grandsons were *today*.'

'Oh, the *old folks' home*. And what interest does ARSE have in that wrinkly old lot? Apart from having wrinkly arses, hahahahaha!' Grandad was loving this, even if he was the only one laughing.

'It's *A-FoRSE*,' the man insisted. 'Like, oh my God, can you just get the name right?'

'I'm getting a pain in my A-FoRSE, that's what I think,' Grandad retorted. 'What do you want with my lads?'

'We're investigating any contact they've had with the residents of the nursing home,' the woman said. 'Sir, this is a matter of national security and we're not at liberty to discuss –'

'*National security*, is it? Who d'you think you're fooling? Think I was born yesterday? And what's with that get-up? Matchin' suits, guys? You look like a pair of arses!'

'Can you please stop with the bottom stuff? It's *A-FoRSE* –'

'"A for Arse", then, or whatever you want to call it. You're not trying to tell me that some old folks in a home and some schoolkids are a threat to national security? And if they are, why is it not the guards or the army calling at this door, instead of a couple of dodgy chancers with fake ID?'

'We showed you our IDs!' the male agent protested. 'These are *real* IDs!'

'Sure, I've never seen a real one, so how would I know if those ones are real or not?' Grandad reasoned with him. 'I've never even heard of any outfit called "A for Arse".'

'It's … it's flippin' *A-FoRSE* – oh my God, you're doing my head in!'

'Here, you don't have anything to do with Francie O'Halloran and his sudden proficiency in the sport of darts, do yiz? Cos if yiz do, you cost me fifty quid!'

'*How much?*' yelled Granny from inside.

'Nothing, dear … Now, look, Special Agent Wife has just caught me out and she didn't need an ARSE suit to do it,' said Grandad.

'Darts? We don't know anything about darts. And if we did, we couldn't say …'

'Right, right.' Grandad tapped the side of his nose. 'National security. *Sure* it is.'

'Look, are the kids here or not?' the other agent tried again.

'That's for me to know and you to find out,' Grandad said firmly. 'If they've been causing any trouble, my wife and I will deal with it. Mostly my wife, really. Not that they have ever caused trouble in the past, and that's exactly why it's a mystery why you are here,' Grandad persisted.

'It's nothing bad – we just want to know who they've been talking to in the nursing home,' the woman replied, her voice tight with frustration. 'Can we please just ask them some questions?'

'So they haven't been causing any trouble then? Because, as I said, they don't cause trouble.'

'No. No, they –'

'Well then, you can take your ARSE suits and your ARSE sunglasses and hop into your big black ARSEmobile and you can FLIP OFF!' Grandad said, and slammed the door shut.

The Five O's scrambled from the bedroom door to the window in time to see the two agents look at one another, give up all hope and head back to their car.

'I never thought I'd say this,' Sive whispered, 'but your grandad is a *god*!

'That was awesome,' Dallan added.

'They shouldn't have called on a Sunday when he was reading his paper,' Derek said. 'They didn't stand a chance, the poor sods.'

They were all a little shaken. Despite Grandad's dismissal of the two agents, it was worrying to think these intimidating, official-looking people had come hunting for the O'Brien brothers. Presumably, they would be searching for the other Five O's too. There was no avoiding this mystery any more. Because now the mystery knew where they lived.

CHAPTER TWELVE:
ART OR CRIME?

There was still some time left that autumn Sunday afternoon, before it started getting dark, to get out and do something ... so Derek told them to get out of the room because he wanted to do himself up. He had friends to meet and a shopping centre to go to. Popping the top on his Lynx Africa, he turned to add a warning as they filed out of the room: 'And don't go saying a word to anyone about this stuff. If you embarrass me in front of my friends with any of this, I'll replace your face with your bum cheeks – remember?'

While Onion, Sive and Dallan decided to head out to the green to play with the drone that had got them mixed up in all of this, Clíona asked if she could have a root around in Onion's attic. She wanted to check something out. Onion said yes, knowing that Granny and Grandad wouldn't mind.

Granny and Grandad's house was the favourite hang-out for the Five O's because they had more freedom there. Parents these days could be very ... *careful* and always wanted to know where their children were. As long as Dallan, Sive and Clíona's parents thought they were hanging around Onion's house, they figured things were fine. However, Granny and Grandad had originally been parents back in the 1970s and 1980s, when parenting was a little different.

Back in the 1980s, kids were expected to be heard, but not seen. They were either somewhere in the house or turfed outside with their friends, and parents kept an ear out when they could, but were otherwise busy with other things. Unless they heard blood-curdling screams or long, suspicious silences, they assumed their children were all right, figuring that if something was badly wrong, *somebody* was bound to come and tell them. Dinner time would eventually draw the little darlings back in, though it was sometimes necessary to go to the front door and shout until the kids either heard you, or the call was passed on down the road by others to the individual being summoned.

The house was also a regular haunt because Granny was a passionate baker, and bakers need people who like to eat freshly baked goods – and the Five O's just happened to be those kinds of people.

Little Molly was young enough to need some supervision, and at that moment, with no hoover to play with, she was still busy painting Granny's toenails – with poster paints. But neither Granny nor Grandad would care much if Clíona wanted to have a look through their attic. She would be suitably out of sight and, knowing Clíona, she would probably fix a few things while she was up there.

In fact, Onion sometimes wished that they could get Clíona to do more jobs about the house. One of the disadvantages of living there was the lack of technology. Derek's pay-as-you-go phone was the only working computer. The credit used up most of his pocket money. There was no Wi-Fi in the house because there was no modem. Yes, they had a *phone*, but it was the type that was actually *plugged into the wall* with a handset that was still attached to the base with one of those twisty cords. Mostly, this lack of tech was because Grandad didn't trust anything he couldn't fix, and he couldn't fix anything designed in this century. And the list of untrustworthy things was getting longer as time went by.

Clíona was also the only one of the four kids who had a phone, though she was constantly fiddling with it, which meant it often didn't work. The drone needed the phone to control it, so she handed it over, and Onion, Sive and Dallan headed out to the green down the road from Onion's house. Sive had the drone tucked under her arm, and they soon had it in the air, buzzing around above them. They weren't just out to have a good time: they were using the drone to see if they could spot any of the People in Black.

It wasn't long before the drone's camera spotted the black van out on Ballinlud Avenue. It was speeding up the road towards the shopping centre. Then they saw the black SUV pull in behind it, and then another one, all of them moving in an awful hurry.

'They're moving with a purpose, aren't they?' Sive said.

Then the phone chimed with a text from Derek – it appeared on the screen over the view from the drone's camera.

'Down at the SC,' the text said. **'GET DOWN HERE. NOW.'**

It took them about five minutes to get there, running the whole way and sending the drone ahead of them. A lot of people had got there before them, too, standing around the near end of the building, including the People in Black. They were hanging back by their black vehicles, all dressed in their signature suits. Elektra McGaffney was looking upwards as she spoke on her phone.

Onion remembered the cherry-picker he'd seen the last time they'd been in the shopping centre – the one the men were using to work on the wide sign over the main door. The machine had been moved around the side to the expansive section of blank wall, nearly two storeys high, that took up most of the end of the building. But it wasn't being controlled by the work crew. An elderly man was up on the platform, using the height to paint a mural on the huge area of wall. Armed with aerosol paints, he was producing the biggest, most impressive piece of graffiti Onion had ever seen.

It was Eoin, the guy from the nursing home, the artist in the motorised wheelchair. He was standing now, though he had to hold onto the guardrail to keep himself steady. His lined, dark-skinned face had an intense expression, as if he had to finish this piece of work no matter what.

And it was some piece of work. Sive burst out laughing and then covered her mouth. Onion was wheezing from the exertion of the run, and he giggled so hard when he saw the graffiti, he had to take a burst of his inhaler. Dallan broke into a wide grin and did a chef's kiss. 'Beautiful, Eoin!' he called out. 'This'll be your masterpiece!'

The painting was nearly finished, and it showed a man who bore a striking resemblance to the CEO of St Brigit's of the Weeping Wound kneeling in front of a toilet, with his hand deep in the bowl. The words in a speech bubble over Austin Leary's head read:

'This bog roll's only been used once! I won't have you wasting it!'

CHAPTER TWELVE: ART OR CRIME?

People were clapping and cheering, for many of them had friends or relatives in the local nursing home. Some of the more mature women, however, were shaking their heads in disgust. Derek and his mates were there too, and he strolled over to Onion. 'The oul' lad's been here for about an hour,' he said. 'Can you believe that picture? I wish I could do something like that for my Junior Cert art. *That's* the kind of stuff they should be teaching us.'

This particular kind of art was, unfortunately, also a crime. Even seriously good artists couldn't just go painting on other people's stuff without permission. The guards had arrived and were trying to impose some order. It was the Ferg and Garda Judge, pushing through the crowd. The Ferg waved at Eoin and called up to him. 'All right now, lad, that's enough! Come on down now. Bring it down.'

Eoin looked over the guardrail and made a pretty rude gesture with his free hand. Onion caught sight of his wrist; the number 6 was written on it in black marker.

'Don't you make me come up there!' the Ferg bellowed at Eoin, his face turning a deep red. He started to try and climb the cherry-picker, but the Ferg wasn't a man who was physically equipped for climbing, so he stopped, slid back down and pointed at his partner. 'Don't make *Garda Judge* come up there!'

Garda Judge had used her head, however, having no intention of climbing up that high to wrestle with an old-age pensioner. She'd called the fire brigade. Now, a fire engine pulled into the car park, the crowd parting before it, and Judge waved them into position. Eoin had completed his masterpiece but didn't want to surrender to the authorities just yet. Seizing the joystick that controlled the base of the cherry-picker, he backed the machine away from the wall, turned it round and drove away, swinging around the back of the building.

CHAPTER THIRTEEN: STICKING IT TO THE MAN

The firefighters set off after Eoin in their truck, and the Ferg jumped on the back. The crowd chased after them on foot, making it all look like some kind of mad parade. The towering vehicle was not very fast, nor was it built for cornering, and it tottered around, coming perilously close to toppling every time Eoin took a tight turn. Garda Judge ran for her patrol car, started the engine and did a skid turn, tyres screaming, before driving off in the opposite direction around the building. Sive sent the drone up into the air because otherwise the kids weren't going to see anything, stuck as they were behind all the adults.

'This is *brilliant*!' Dallan exclaimed, as they hurried after the fugitive cherry-picker.

Judge tried to block the cherry-picker's path as it came around the far end of the shopping centre,

but Eoin had just enough space to wobble around her car, and he gave another rude gesture before roaring up the car park, heading slowly for the exit at the far end. The fire engine was blaring its sirens now, as it gave chase in a very low gear. At the far end of the car park, close to where he'd started, Eoin found that exit blocked by a black van, and when he tried to do another lap of the building, he was blocked by a black SUV. People were whooping and cheering, this being one of the most exciting things ever to happen in this shopping centre, and Eoin grinned and waved at the crowd as he backed away from the SUV and swung in closer to the building.

Top 5 Most Exciting Things to Happen at Ballinlud Shopping Centre

1. That time Eoin Macken painted a huge piece of graffiti on the wall and tried to escape from the guards and the fire brigade in a cherry-picker

2. When *Riverdance* was performed in the middle of the mall by local amateurs – hilarious: there was literally no room, and they ended up riverdancing on top of each other

3. When a freak snowstorm happened, and whoever was in there at the time got free sweets and cakes until it stopped

4. The time Dicky Dolan, the famous singer, came to perform, but halfway through his set his wig fell off into the crowd, they thought it was a rat and it caused a stampede

5. That time Mitchin' Mick, the professional snooker player, was doing his shopping and had to hit a crazed fan with a fresh salmon when the stalker wouldn't leave him alone

CHAPTER THIRTEEN: STICKING IT TO THE MAN

Edging the cherry-picker up to the wall of the building, Eoin raised the platform until it was level with the roof and then clambered up onto the roof itself. He didn't look steady on his feet, and the slight slope of the tiles seemed too much for him. Even so, he looked determined to make a last stand.

'Oh, please God, don't let him FALL!' Sive gasped, nearly swallowing her gum in fright.

Even as she said it, Eoin slipped and fell on the tiles, sliding down slightly, but not enough to bring him close to the edge. He got up on his hands and knees and started crawling towards the top.

'This is mental,' Onion said. 'What's he trying to do?'

'Make it last,' Derek said. 'He's sticking it to the Man and he wants to make the moment last. He's a rebel, and I think he's *the flippin' bomb*.'

'Who's "the man"?' Onion asked.

'The *Man*,' Derek repeated, looking at his brother as if he was stupid. He gestured to the guards and the People in Black and the shopping-centre staff. 'The – the – system. The authorities who control everything. This is a rebellion, and I am *absolutely* here for it.'

Onion seriously doubted that Derek was here for any rebellion unless it could be carried out on his phone. Derek wasn't one to put too much effort into anything, but Eoin was certainly rebelling against something because he was standing up on the roof of the building shouting curses down at the guards and the firefighters who were raising their ladder to come after him.

Just as it was looking like the firefighters might actually have to climb up the roof after the elderly man, a black helicopter swooped into view over the nearby houses. A woman was hanging from a cable underneath it. And though she was wearing a helmet and the harness covered up some of her black suit, the Five O's could see it was Elektra McGaffney. The chopper glided in smoothly, the wind making Eoin crouch down so he wouldn't get blown over.

'Look, it's the – what the – who – LOOK, LOOK!' Onion cried out.

As everyone watched in amazement, the helicopter swung in. McGaffney grabbed Eoin, clipped a safety harness around him and a winch hauled them both up to the open door of the helicopter. They were pulled inside and the door slid shut. Moments later, the chopper was flying off, a shrinking dot in the cloudy sky.

'Did you – did anyone see that?' Onion gaped at the disappearing aircraft. His whole body was shaking. 'What … what was that? The thing, woman, she took the fella – where did they …?'

'OK,' Derek said, shrugging. 'OK, so … so maybe something weird *is* going on at that old folks' home.'

They hung around for a while longer, but nothing else was going to happen. The Ferg looked stunned, Garda Judge looked ready to kill someone, the People in Black had disappeared and the fire brigade had gone back to the station. Deciding that the drama was well and truly over, the four core members of the Five O's brought their drone down and started the walk home. Derek stayed on with his mates because the shopping centre was still the place to be, even when nobody was flying around the car park in a cherry-picker.

'We got it on video this time,' Sive said. 'Wait'll Clíona sees it – she's going to be so mad she missed it.'

The phone rang, flashing up the O'Briens' home number. It was Clíona.

CHAPTER THIRTEEN: STICKING IT TO THE MAN

'You guys, you've got to get back here!' she said breathlessly. 'I've found something. I think ... I think I've found where I've seen Alexander before. This could be huge!'

'Yeah, we're getting that feeling,' Sive replied. 'We've got a bit of news ourselves. We'll be back in a few minutes. Listen ... don't say anything more on the phone, OK? Especially about Alexander. Somebody could be listening in. Don't talk to anyone until we figure this out.'

She ended the call, then nearly dropped the phone when a voice said from behind them: 'Figure what out? And what's that about Alexander?'

Standing right there, right behind the Five O's, were Tina Dalton and the Bang-Off-Them Brothers. They were all dressed in black suits and Tina had her wavy blonde locks tied back in a businesslike ponytail.

'What's this?' Sive asked. 'You off to a funeral?'

'Oh. Hilarious,' Tina said in a flat, very unamused voice. 'No. Our services have been engaged by ...

well, let's just call them "an interested party". And they're *interested* in what *you've* been doing down at that old folks' home … And, especially, what you might know about an *Alexander Yuryev*.'

CHAPTER FOURTEEN:
THE OLD RUSSIAN'S
SECRET

Alarm bells started ringing in Onion's head and he felt a desire to suck on his inhaler. If the People in Black had got Tina and the brothers involved, it could mean bad news for someone. Or everyone. Tina's kind of trouble had a way of spreading itself around.

'We don't know anything about any oul' Russian fella,' he said immediately, trying to stop his wonky eye from waving around like a flag. Tina knew his eye's treacherous ways.

'I never said he was *Russian*,' she said with sweet smile, cold as an ice-pop.

'Well ... with a name like Yuryev ...' Onion stammered. 'He's obviously –'

'Shush, Onion,' Dallan said, then he added with a smirk, 'So, Tina, does this mean you're working for ARSE now?'

'What's that?' she asked, in a tone that promised torment.

Dallan's smile disappeared. 'Eh, noth– nothing. It was just a ... a kind of joke. Although ... if it's the old folks' home you're interested in, we can tell you *all sorts* of things about the people there.'

'No, no, no! I don't want *you* to start talking!' Tina snapped, raising a finger at him. 'Not you.'

CHAPTER FOURTEEN: THE OLD RUSSIAN'S SECRET

'There's Mrs Tunstall,' Dallan began, 'who's got an ear for the gossip, was a bit of a tearaway in her day, liked a spin on a motorbike from time to time and is addicted to custard creams –'

'I said *don't.*'

'Or Pixel Pat, who used to run the arcade and programmed some of the first computer games in Ireland, but didn't have a girlfriend until he was forty-three. He takes his tea so strong he has to paint his false teeth white when they're too hard to clean –'

'OK, seriously, I want you to shut up!' Tina tried again, but Dallan was only getting into his stride.

'– And then there's Ursula,' he continued, 'who was a pole vaulter and a cake decorator and could take your head off with a spinning kick or carve your face in marzipan when she was in her prime, though she prefers a bit of a disco these days –'

'Oh, HOLY GOD! You will shut your gob or I'll have one of my boys swing you round by your tongue!' Tina snarled.

'– Or there's Eoin, who used to do cartoons for newspapers and painted the ads for the sides of buses and can't walk too well because of his bad hips, but he's totally in love with Ursula and he's never told her, although *everyone* knows and they wish he'd do something about it –'

'I'm losing the will to live.' Tina groaned, putting her hands to her face. 'Plant him, lads.'

The Bang brothers stepped around their goddess, Barry clamping his hands around Dallan's head to cover his mouth, as Larry lifted his fist to clout the smaller boy on the top of the skull. Tina thumped her fist into her hand and Dallan flinched, but Sive quickly held up Clíona's phone, took a photo and tapped the screen.

'Go for it, lads,' she said. 'By all means, thump away. But I just sent that photo to my school account, so if Dallan comes into school tomorrow with bruises, I can show Ms Lemon how it happened.'

The two bullies paused, looking to Tina for further orders. Ms Lemon was the principal of their school and not someone to be messed with. While the Bang brothers had no problem with getting in trouble, Tina's record was immaculate, and she was very particular about keeping it that way. Adults thought Tina was the perfect young lady, mainly because nobody could provide any proof to the contrary. She was very careful about leaving evidence.

'You get a stay of execution then,' she said at last, straightening her black tie and sliding her fingertips along her gorgeous tied-back blonde hair. 'But don't think that photo can protect you for long.'

And with that, she walked away, and the brothers shoved Dallan to the ground and hurried after her.

'Maybe …' Sive muttered. 'But maybe it'll be just long enough.'

The three Five O's made a quick retreat to Onion's house, where they found Clíona had taken command of the video recorder in the living room.

This was a machine that still played VHS video tapes, which was a kind of medium that recorded video onto a plastic tape winding between two spools in a black case the size of a paperback book. Clíona already had a tape in the machine, and she showed them the cover.

'*This* is where I've seen Alexander before,' she said, a big geeky grin on her face as she pressed Play.

Onion recognised the cover. It was from a documentary series called *Strange Ways to Die*, which had been released back in the 1980s. Grandad had found the whole box set years ago in an old cupboard in one of the places where he worked as a handyman.

Clíona had been badly bullied in school when she was younger. Her mum was a scientist and Clíona shared a lot of her nerdy interests, including a passion for ancient technology. Not long after he'd met her, Onion had told her about the video recorder, and she'd asked to see it. From that point on, when things were bad for her, Onion would bring her home with him after school and they'd sit and watch old videos on this antique machine. They'd watched this whole series, all twelve shows.

Granny, Grandad and Molly were in the room too this evening, since Clíona had interrupted the six o'clock news. Grandad wasn't too happy, though he'd been stuck behind his newspaper at the time anyway. Granny was knitting and Molly was playing with a ball of wool.

This episode was about Russia, or rather the Soviet Union, the group of countries that Russia had ruled back then. The programme's deeply tanned American presenter, with his stiff, swept-back hair, was some actor from an extinct science fiction show.

'There are many dangers in life,' he began, with the usual introduction, his voice dark with drama. 'And we're here tonight to look at some of the weirdest. These stories are not for the timid, not for the faint of heart. They will quicken your pulse and chill your blood. And tonight, we're taking you to the Soviet Union for the latest episode of ... *Strange Ways to Die!*'

'OK, I'm going to skip past this next bit,' Clíona said. 'I like the intro, but this is all about oil-rig workers and the guys who drive on the ice highways. It's gruesome, but it's not what we're here for. Molly, you might not want to watch this – it's a bit scary.'

'I *like* scary!' Molly declared.

'Let's go make a cup of tea and a glass of strawberry milk, love,' Granny said. 'Remember how you got nightmares after that drinking-and-driving advert? It might be like that.'

'Oh, ooohhhkay ...'

Clíona pressed the Fast Forward button, and the grainy video whizzed through a bunch of reports of horrible work accidents until it came to a scene that looked like something out of a 1960s science fiction show, much like the one the presenter had starred in.

'This is the story of Dr Yury Alexeyev, a brilliant physicist who was working in one of Russia's top scientific institutes back in 1978. He was part of the team working on an experimental particle accelerator ...'

'What's a particle accelerator?' Onion asked.

Clíona paused the video, regarded him for a few seconds and took a breath, wondering how to break this down for him and the others. 'A particle accelerator is a tunnel that runs in a circle,' she explained. 'It's made for firing charged particles, such as protons or electrons, in beams of energy at high speeds – sometimes close to *light* speed. They basically smash atomic particles together to see what happens to them. Some of these facilities are huge; there's a place in Switzerland that has a circular tunnel twenty-seven kilometres long. They're used for carrying out research in particle physics.'

'OK, got it,' Onion said quickly, and the other two Five O's nodded.

None of them had, in fact, *got it*, but they'd immediately recognised that they weren't going to get it, and that was what they had Clíona for after all – to understand techy science stuff on their behalf. Clíona rewound a bit and then pressed the Play button again. The film showed photos of the research facility with a long, long tube that disappeared down the middle of a curving tunnel. The colour didn't look realistic, almost like someone had coloured in the photos, and all the people had bad hairstyles and glasses and were dressed in boring clothes and white coats. They were very definitely scientists.

CHAPTER FOURTEEN: THE OLD RUSSIAN'S SECRET

'... He was part of the team working on an experimental particle accelerator when *something terrible went wrong*!' the presenter said in an ominous tone. 'While Alexeyev was leaning in through a hatch to check a malfunctioning part, the machine somehow activated, despite all the safety procedures.

'The particle beam was fired down the tunnel, and Alexeyev's head was caught in the beam. Because the research they were conducting was *top secret*, his death was covered up by the Russian authorities, and no one knows what became of his body.

'Rumours abound. Some say that he was vaporised instantly, and there was no body to recover. Others claim his ghost haunts the facility and is sometimes picked up by the cameras inside the tunnel. Some even say that just his head was vaporised, while his body was turned into a weapon and used for spy missions against America in the Cold War.

'But to this day, Dr Yury Alexeyev remains the only man to be killed by a particle beam accelerator.'

The last shot was of Alexeyev, taken not long before the accident. He was handsome, in a bland, square-faced sort of way, with a wild shock of black hair and intense eyes.

And the Five O's had no doubt they were looking at a photo of a young Alexander Yuryev, the seemingly lifeless man in St Brigit's of the Weeping Wound with the strange scar on his face.

CHAPTER FIFTEEN: —
SUMMONED INTO THE DARKNESS

I t seemed incredible that a story that had started
in some research facility back in Russia in the
late seventies should find itself here, in an old
folks' home in *Ballinlud*. Could Alexander Yuryev,
that still figure in the wheelchair, really be the
brilliant physicist Dr Yury Alexeyev? The presenter
said the man was dead, but the resemblance couldn't
be denied, even given all the years that had passed.
And the accident would explain Alexander's scar.
Had he been in this frozen state ever since? And
if that was so, how had he ended up in Ireland?

And if all this was true, what exactly was the People in Black's interest in him?

'What kind of eejit sticks his head into a big laser beam?' Grandad said, jolting them all out of their pondering. 'I mean, if I was working on a laser beam, the first thing I wouldn't do is stick my head in there. In fact, I've worked on a laser beam before,' Grandad said proudly.

'No, you haven't, Paddy. You're talking about the time you replaced the fluorescent lighting in the local parish hall,' explained Granny as she returned to the room with Molly, who now had a strawberry milk moustache.

'Same thing, and you didn't see me putting me head in them, like that gob daw,' answered Paddy.

'Strictly speaking, it was an accident,' Clíona pointed out. 'The safety measures failed.'

'Still stuck his head in there, though, didn't he, the fool,' Grandad insisted. 'He's getting lion taming mixed up with laser fitting – you stick your head in a lion's mouth as a tamer, but you defo don't stick your head into a laser, the Russian twist!'

'God help me,' pleaded Granny with her eyes to the sky.

'I wonder what that would do to your brain?' Dallan said.

'*Roast* it, probably,' Sive answered. 'You can see the state of him.'

'I'm not sure he's as gone as everyone thinks he is,' Onion said. 'I've looked in his eyes. There's still something in there. I think … I think he might be putting it on. Or, at least, he's not as – as – as … oh, I don't know what you call it … paralysed?'

'Catatonic,' Clíona said.

'OK … yeah, he's not as *catatonic* as he looks.'

'That's how I was last Xmas Eve,' giggled Grandad.

'Paddy!' shouted Granny.

'He looked pretty catatonic to me,' Dallan said, delighted with the new word.

'That's your diagnosis, is it, Dr Dallan?' Sive asked. 'Look, I don't know, Onion. When I saw

Alexander, he had dribble coming out the side of his mouth. I don't think anyone would sit there and dribble if they could stop it, so I don't think there's anyone home in there, but everything else about this is so weird, well ... I mean, who knows? The thing is, what's he got to do with everything else that's going on there? Because it's got to be connected, right?'

Everyone nodded. It *had* to be connected. But how?

'It's like I said before, it's a retirement home for spies,' Sive said, popping some fresh gum in her mouth. 'I mean, a Russian scientist who's presumed dead and then shows up alive years later with a scar on his face? Come on, he's *totally* an ex-spy.'

'But then how do the aliens fit into this?' Dallan asked.

'There are no flippin' aliens!' Sive said in an exasperated voice. 'There's no such thing as aliens.'

'Oh, sure, but *Russian spies* in Ballinlud are so realistic,' he retorted, folding his arms and scowling.

CHAPTER FIFTEEN: SUMMONED INTO THE DARKNESS

'Maybe it's a retirement home for eejits,' Grandad said from behind his newspaper. 'Now go on upstairs, the lot of yeh. I'm trying to read.'

It was getting close to dinner time anyway, so Sive, Dallan and Clíona headed off home. Onion played back the video and watched the piece on the scientist again. Some of the photos shown on the screen while the presenter talked were of newspaper reports of the accident. They were mostly in Russian, so they made no sense to Onion, but there was one in an American paper. Because it was in English, it caught his eye, and he paused the video to look at it more carefully.

VHS tapes weren't very good at pausing; the picture was fuzzy and flickered a bit, but he could read some of the lines in the article. One line in particular stood out: 'Russian authorities insist there is no truth to the rumours that the damage was self-inflicted, that Alexeyev was carrying out experiments on the effects of microwaves on brain cells as part of some secret Soviet super-soldier programme.'

Onion had heard about super-soldier programmes. It came up in Hollywood action films all the time. There was always some story or other about places like America or Russia trying to make their soldiers stronger or faster or smarter. He looked at the words 'self-inflicted'. That meant that Alexeyev had done it to himself *on purpose*. That he'd willingly stuck his head into a big energy beam. If that was true, what was it he was trying to do?

Maybe Grandad was right. Maybe the man was an eejit.

Still, it was just a line in a random newspaper on a dodgy documentary show back in the eighties – probably a load of rubbish. Onion kept turning it around in his head and he finally admitted to himself that he didn't know enough about this stuff to figure it out. He'd talk to Clíona about it tomorrow.

Derek was home just in time for dinner, and much of the conversation at the table was about Eoin and his mad chase around the shopping centre. Granny didn't know what to make of it at all, at all, and Grandad said there was no telling what a man might do if he was pushed too far.

Onion wondered if this meant that some day Grandad might go out and hijack a cherry-picker if things got too much for him, but decided it was unlikely. When things got too much for him, Grandad took to his armchair, stuck his bare feet in a basin of hot water and Dettol and sought refuge behind his newspaper. It had worked for him for years and he wasn't about to change his habits now.

It was late when Onion and Derek got to bed, and Derek conked out and started snoring as soon as he'd burrowed into his bed, having had a hard day hanging out at the shopping centre. Onion lay awake, his head fizzing with thoughts. He'd never be able to sleep if he couldn't calm his brain down.

That was why he was still awake after midnight when he heard a whirring sound from the floor at the bottom of his bed. It was a strange buzzing electronic noise, and it was growing louder. It wasn't loud, but it was definitely *there*. Frozen in fear, Onion peered over the top of his duvet, down past his toes, as something rose up in the darkness, its edges flickering slightly. His first thought was that it was some kind of ghost. Then he thought it might be some kind of killer robot, sent by the People in Black to attack him in his sleep.

Then his eyes made sense of the shape and, though his fear subsided slightly, he remained thoroughly freaked out.

It was Clíona's drone, which she'd left in the bedroom. And it had just started itself up and was hovering over his bed, hanging in the air with its four sets of spinning rotors, its camera aimed at the boy in the bed, like a beady little eye. He reasoned that this *could* be Clíona working it with her phone, but she wasn't the type to try and scare Onion in the middle of the night, and she'd know that this would scare the bejaypers out of him. Maybe she'd forgotten where she'd left it and, thinking she'd lost it, she was trying to fly it home?

Then the drone flew up closer to his face and did a kind of flick of its nose towards the bedroom door. It flew over to the door and did the flick again. Onion stuck a hand out from under the duvet and pointed towards the door. 'You want me to follow you?' he asked softly.

The drone nodded – or, at least, did its version of a nod. Onion sat up and glanced over at Derek, who was still fast asleep and snoring like a pig with a head cold.

'Derek!' he called out in a slightly louder voice. **'Derek, wake up! You need to see this!'**

His older brother snorted, muttered something rude and went back to snoring. The drone flew right up to Onion's face and shook itself. It looked annoyed.

'Oh … OK. OK,' Onion whispered, putting a hand to his chest. 'You want me to come alone?'

It nodded again.

'Are … are you Clíona?'

The drone shook itself and did the flick towards the door, acting impatient – if that was even possible for a drone. He should have woken Derek. He should have run screaming past the drone and called out for Granny and Grandad. He did neither of these things, partly because he was too terrified not to do what it was telling him, and partly because he thought that, if he followed the drone, he might find out what was going on. Caught between fear and curiosity, Onion slipped out of bed and quickly got dressed.

He took a deep breath, which felt a bit wheezy, so he took a drag on his inhaler and then nodded to the hovering machine. 'OK, then. Let's go.'

CHAPTER SIXTEEN:
FLY BY NIGHT

The drone led Onion down Ballinlud Avenue, high enough that it was above the glow of the streetlights while still staying in Onion's sight. It wasn't moving very fast, so he could walk at a normal pace, though it would still look odd for a kid his age to be out on his own at that time of night – not that this would be the first time.

It wasn't long before he realised that someone was following him. They weren't keeping their footsteps very quiet, and when he looked back, they weren't hard to spot. This was because Barry Bang was far too large to hide behind a lamp-post, which he did in a rush as Onion turned around.

And if one Bang brother was too large to hide behind a lamp-post, then two of them trying to hide behind the *same* lamp-post made no sense at all.

They were about twenty metres behind him, still dressed in their black suits, and he was careful not to react. Instead, he kept walking, looking behind him every now and then in time to see them dive in through a gateway or throw themselves over a wall – sometimes with a satisfyingly solid thud or cry of pain. Onion was thankful they were trying to be sly, rather than just running after him and beating the stuffing out of him, but he suspected they'd give up on stealth sooner or later and do what came more naturally.

The drone led him to the field behind his school, St Hilarius National School. This took him off the road and away from the streetlights. The dark made him nervous. He followed the machine across to the Valley, the stretch of waste ground that ran along either side of the stream known as the Big Leak. At the far end of the field, it was very dark, yet the Bang-Off-Them Brothers had nothing to hide behind now as they followed him across the stretch of grass.

In one awful moment, Onion looked back and saw them, and they saw him looking, and he saw the looks on their faces as they realised that he was looking at them, and now nobody could pretend that they didn't know what was going on, and the brothers gave up on the stealth approach right then and charged at the smaller boy. Their combined weight in muscle, along with the speed achieved by their big pounding legs, was like a rhino charging a sheep. Onion did the only thing he could do … He ran for his life, over the bank of grass that ran along the edge of the Valley, tripping and stumbling in the gloom down the path on the bank of the stream and then into the darkness of the trees that lay at the end of the strip of wasteland.

Even following the path, the ground was rough, littered with rocks and roots and other things he couldn't see. Twice, he stubbed his toe – the *same* toe – on rocks, and another time, he nearly took his head off hitting it against a low-hanging branch. He let out a yelp and tried not to cry as he clutched at the pain. He could still hear the drone a little way ahead of him, lower now so that he could keep track of it. He knew where it was taking him, of course. Towards the old folks' home. It had to be Pixel Pat, hacking the drone again.

As he walked face-first into another leafy branch, Onion hoped this would all be worth it.

At this rate, he'd end up beating himself up before the brothers could even catch him. He stubbed his other toe against a root, hopped around in pain and then fell over the trunk of a fallen tree. He could hear the big thugs crashing through the undergrowth towards him, not even bothering to follow the path, just bashing their way through to him.

'We'll find you, O'Brien! You should come out now! The harder you make this, the harder this'll be on you! We saw that drone! We just want to know about the Russian! You're facing a world of pain, you little guzzer!'

Onion groaned and got to his feet. With both of his big toes bruised, running was harder, but he saw light ahead now. Jogging across the small clearing, he could see the trees that backed onto the nursing home. The drone was heading off to the right, and he continued to follow it, taking shallow, painful breaths as he ran. The brothers were still stomping through the woods behind him, with all the grace of a pair of elephants walking on their hind legs.

Coming to the wall, he found a tree that had grown up against it, a convenient ladder that led to the top and onto the roof of a shed on the other side. From there, Onion was able to climb down onto a row of big wheelie bins standing in a fenced-off yard that separated the small car park in the front from the nursing home's back garden.

Panting for breath, he leaned against the door of the shed and took a hurried blast of his inhaler. The drone was higher now, flying over the back garden. He was about to follow it when he heard a voice from the other side of the tall gate.

'... I don't know, I keep *taking* the thing and, somehow, he keeps getting it back! It's inconceivable!' It was Austin Leary, and he was talking on his phone. 'Now I can't find it at all! You can tell McGaffney if she's so keen to get her hands on that notebook, she can come and find it herself. I'M NOT HER SLAVE!'

CHAPTER SIXTEEN: FLY BY NIGHT

The gate was opening. Onion clambered back up onto one of the wide wheelie bins as quietly as he could, intending to climb back over the wall.

'I don't care what she says ...' Leary was growling. Then he tittered nervously. '... What? No. No! *Of course* I don't want you to tell her that. Ha ha! Seriously, *please* don't tell her that ...'

As he reached for the wall, Onion heard the Bang brothers noisily climbing the tree on the other side, huffing and puffing after their stomp through the woods, moments away from reaching the top of the wall. He had nowhere to go.

With only seconds to make a decision, he scrambled across the lid of one wheelie bin, pulled up the lid of the one next to it and dived in, letting the lid drop shut behind him. He almost immediately regretted this decision, as the smell of different kinds of chemicals nearly started him coughing, the fumes strong enough to make his head spin. All around him he could feel bits of cloth of different sizes and plastic bags and packaging and plastic containers, and most of it was wet and everything stank.

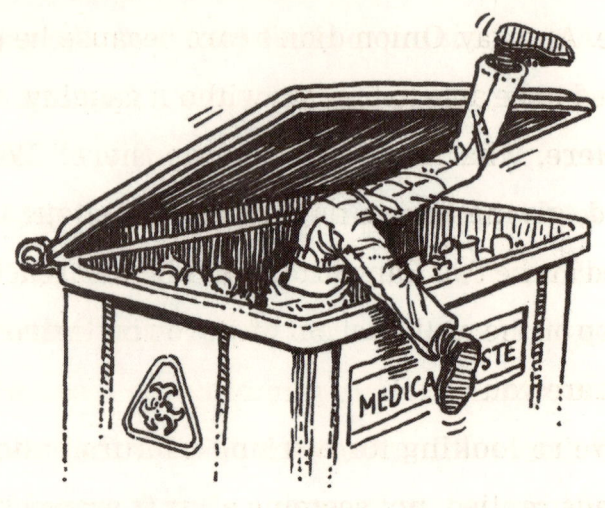

He remembered hearing somewhere that any place that dealt with sick people had to have special bins for medical waste, to keep it separate from normal rubbish, because there was really nasty stuff in medical waste like out-of-date medicines and toxic cleaning chemicals and even worse things. He wondered if he was in one of those bins now, or if the nursing home even had one of those bins, because they'd cost extra and Austin Leary didn't seem to be the kind of guy who paid extra for anything. No, this was probably a bin full of *everything* that could be thrown out from a nursing home. Anyway, Onion didn't care because he just wanted to be able to breathe without gagging.

'Here, what are you doing up there!' Leary yelled, giving him a fright, but the shout was aimed at the two Bang brothers, who had reached the top of the wall. 'Get out of it, you little thieves! What are you up to?'

'We're looking for a friend of ours,' one of the lads replied, not seeming all that scared. 'We thought he came in here.'

'Inconceivable! You've no friends in here! Get lost before I call the guards! I'm calling them now!'

Several of the hard-edged plastic containers were sticking into Onion's legs and bum and, trying to get more comfortable, he put his hand in something that was soft and squishy and he felt the sudden need to throw up. He didn't, because a new smell stabbed up his nostrils and brought tears to his eyes, and suddenly he forgot about vomiting as he clamped the clean hand over his nose. It smelled like something had died, started to rot, had been cleaned with bleach, soaked in sewage and then sprayed with deodorant. Onion wondered if this was what you smelled when you died and went to hell.

'Bloody kids,' Leary muttered as he opened the lid on Onion's bin.

Onion had his eyes tightly closed, waiting for the moment when he'd be dragged out, but instead, three plastic bags of rubbish were dumped on top of him and the bin slammed shut again. He heard the gate of the yard open and shut, and then he listened for another minute to make sure Leary was gone. He was about to push the lid up when he heard the gate again. This time, the footsteps were quieter, more careful. One foot dragged slightly, and the person's breathing was rough and wheezy. The limping footsteps came right over to Onion's bin and stopped, less than a metre from where he crouched in the garbage.

CHAPTER SIXTEEN: FLY BY NIGHT

Then the man seized the lid and threw it open, and Onion opened his eyes to find himself staring up into the scarred face of Alexander Yuryev.

CHAPTER SEVENTEEN:
—
A SECRET RENDEZVOUS

Yuryev, or Alexeyev, or whatever his name was, held his hand out to Onion, who took it, and the man helped drag him out of the bin. Onion wiped himself down as best he could, and then Alexander gestured to him to follow and went through the gate to the back garden.

He led Onion to a dark spot between some bushes and the fence where the drone had landed, out of sight of the building. Onion looked around warily. If the man tried anything here, Onion would be a long way from any help. But they were also less likely to be interrupted by another appearance from Austin Leary.

'Your name is Onion, yes?' the man said softly in a heavy accent. 'I am Alexander.'

'Are you … are you also Dr Yury Alexeyev from Russia?' Onion asked.

The man's disfigured face seemed caught off guard for a moment, and then he nodded. 'So you know. Yes, I am Alexeyev. How did you find out?'

'From an old TV show,' Onion replied, babbling because he was shivering with nerves. 'My grandad found this old box set in this place he worked a few years back and I watched it with my friend, Clíona …'

'Clíona,' Alexander said, 'now *she* seems like an intelligent child.' His tone implied that she might be the only one who was.

'… And she remembered and your face reminded her of his face,' Onion continued, 'the man's face in the video, I mean, not my grandad's face – and we thought it might be you and that maybe this was a retirement home for spies or aliens or superhuman mutants or whatever and –'

'Perhaps you could tell me all about it another time.' Alexander interrupted him, holding up his hand. He looked at the time on his chunky steel digital watch, then over his shoulder towards the nursing home. 'I only have a few minutes, and I –' He sniffed the air and then coughed. 'This … this is a most remarkable smell you have. It is like someone ate too much garlic and then vomited on a skunk.'

'It's from the *bin*,' Onion explained. 'The bin I ended up in because I was following that drone.'

'Yes, thank you for that,' Alexander said, taking

a step backwards from the boy and waving away the air in front of him. 'My friend Pixel arranged that for me. I know it was a strange way to make contact. I brought you out here because you and your grandmother and your friends seem honest and kind and I need help, and I have no one I can trust on the outside.'

Onion wasn't sure how honest or kind he and his friends were, though this didn't seem the time to say it. He supposed they tried their best, which was all that most people could do. The old man was clearly desperate if he had to use a drone to bring a kid to the garden of his nursing home in the middle of the night. There were surely easier ways to ask for help, even if everyone did think you were some catatonic guy in a wheelchair.

'The woman, Elektra McGaffney, and her people are trying to get their hands on this notebook.' Alexander held up the book in question. 'It contains important scientific research, work that has taken my whole life to put together. I cannot explain what it's about right now. It is very advanced and complicated –'

'Is it to do with using energy waves to make your brain work better?' Onion asked.

Alexander stared at him for a second. 'Yes, it is,' he said. 'Did you see that on the television too?'

'Yeah.'

'Clearly, I am not watching enough television.' Alexander looked over towards the building again. 'We do not have great television in St Brigit's. Yes, I was working for the Russian government and faked my death so I could escape. They wanted to use my research to experiment on people, to turn them into soldiers and slaves, so I disappeared. I came to Ireland, where they would never think to look. *Nobody* came here back then. In the 1970s, Ireland was almost as depressing as Russia.'

'Is this all real?' Onion asked. 'I mean … it's all very … y'know … science-fiction.'

'It *is* real,' Alexander assured him. 'You've *seen* them in their sunglasses and black suits and black cars and being all secretive. Normal people don't act like that. Anyway, that greedy fool, Leary, knows some of my background. He knows there is valuable information in my notebook. I've been trying to hide it from him, but he keeps finding it. For the moment, he and rest of the staff are fooled by my act that my mind is gone, so he thinks no one knows what he's doing. And while he knows my notes are valuable, he doesn't understand them. So up until now, he didn't know what to do with the notebook or who he could sell it to.'

Top 5 Things Austin Leary Thinks the Notebook Might Contain

1. The secret formula for reusable toilet roll.

2. The secret formula for an ever-lasting bikky.

3. The secret formula for transforming old people's poo into electricity.

4. The secret formula for transforming old people's farts into heating.

5. The secret formula for all secret formulas.

'Did some of the old people find your notes too?' Onion piped up again. 'Is that what's been happening – old people are reading your notebook and figuring out how to zap their brains into being better?'

'That's – no, that's not possible, what you're saying.' The man sighed. 'Nobody is having their brains zapped in an old folks' home. This is just old people acting up because they are so bored in this terrible place. Pay no attention to these things – they are not important. Please listen, I haven't much time.'

'I'm a kid,' Onion said. 'Mrs Tunstall being able to do a wheelie on a motorbike is pretty important to me.'

'Please *listen*. Now *McGaffney* knows about the notebook, and she is a very dangerous person. She must not get her hands on it, but she *will* find it eventually if I keep it here. McGaffney is like my masters in Russia: she knows *exactly* what she wants to do with it. Leary just thinks he can get money for it, but she wants to brainwash people to create soldiers and slaves. I cannot let that happen.'

'Why don't you just leave if you're not stuck in the wheelchair?' Onion asked, gesturing at the man. 'You can walk and talk. Why don't you just walk out of here and disappear, like you did before?'

'Because it takes time to arrange these things, and my mind is failing,' the Russian said, tapping his head, his voice croaking with emotion. 'The beam from the particle accelerator changed my brain. That frozen man in the wheelchair, that is how I am sometimes, and it is happening more and more. Only sometimes am I awake and alert like I am now. I can't go far on my own. My research can help people, but I need to find some honest scientists to help me, who will use it for good, not like McGaffney and her people. Will you take the notebook and hide it?' he begged Onion, holding out the book. 'Keep it somewhere safe – at least until I can get away from McGaffney and find someone who will continue my work?'

Onion gazed down at the leather-bound book being handed to him. He thought about Tina and the Bang-Off-Them Brothers, about that cheapskate, nasty piece of work Austin Leary. He thought about Elektra McGaffney and her black-suited agents and their strange secret organisation. Every bit of sense in him was screaming at him to stay out of this, that he was in way over his head, that this could dump him in more trouble than he'd ever known.

But Alexander thought he was honest and kind, and he was an old man who needed help.

'Yeah, OK,' Onion said, taking the book. 'I'll do it.'

CHAPTER EIGHTEEN: — WEIRD SCIENCE

Onion and Derek both woke late, and no sooner was he out of bed than Derek sniffed the air, leaned in to sniff Onion and nearly gagged.

'Oh my God, you *stink*!' he said, coughing and spraying some Lynx Africa over his brother. 'What did you do last night – go out on the green and roll around in fox poo?'

Onion rubbed his eyes, coughed in the fumes of deodorant and winced at the sudden pain in his bruised toes, slowly remembering the chase through the darkness. And being stuck in the bin at the nursing home. And the drone. And the walking, talking Alexander Yuryev, also known as Dr Yury Alexeyev. And the notebook. As Derek was getting dressed in his school uniform, Onion lifted his pillow. The top secret notebook was still there. He felt a thrill of danger just at the sight of it, yet he knew he had to find a safer place for it. He didn't want Granny coming in and finding it.

He took a quick shower and then dressed in a rush, carefully putting the notebook into his schoolbag as soon as he came downstairs. Wolfing down some cereal for breakfast, he was about to kiss Granny goodbye when she held up a hand.

'We're going to do some more dancing lessons for the folks over at St Brigit's this evening. See if any of your friends want to come, OK?'

Onion nodded, kissed her cheek and ran out the door. He wanted to make sure he got to talk to his friends on the walk to school. The other three Five O's were waiting by the corner on the green, as usual, and he almost burst with all the news that came flowing out as soon as he reached them.

'*You took the notebook?*' Sive cried, spitting out her gum as soon as his outburst was over.

'The thing the *People in Black* are hunting for?' Dallan added, clutching his hair. 'The people who kidnapped a guy and flew him away in a helicopter – you know, *those* people?'

'It has his *research* in it?' Clíona exclaimed, not focusing so much on the negatives. '**Holy cow!** Can I read it?'

'Sure,' Onion said, opening the zip on his bag. 'I had a look, but it's like alien writing to me.'

'Don't take it out here, you idiot!' Sive snapped. 'Do you want someone to see?'

'Man, we've got to get rid of that thing,' said Dallan. 'It's like having a bomb in your schoolbag. If Elektra McGaffney finds out we've got this book, she could make us all disappear. That's what they do to people. You have to give it back, Onion.'

'I can't. I said I'd keep it safe,' Onion told them.

'So you're bringing it to *school*?' Sive groaned, throwing her hands up. '**School isn't safe!**

It's full of children. Valuable stuff is never safe around children. *Tina Bleedin' Dalton* is at school. You can't even keep *yourself* safe at school, let alone some Russian genius's secret science notebook!'

'Keep your voice down!' Onion said.

'*You* keep your voice down! Last night, the Bang brothers chased you from here all the way to the old folks' home because of that Russian and *they're at school* and now you're taking his secret notebook **TO THE SCHOOL!** I can't believe it, one of my best friends is going to get me disappeared. Don't tell me to keep my voice down!'

CHAPTER EIGHTEEN: WEIRD SCIENCE

'I'm not getting anyone disappeared,' Onion argued, though he was starting to see that he might have messed up and maybe they would all be disappeared if they were found with the notebook, and he was feeling a bit stupid about it.

'Maybe we should show the teachers,' Dallan suggested. 'Hand it over to the adults. Mrs Doyle is into science. She might understand it.'

'We are so *not* showing this to a teacher,' Sive said. 'Mrs Doyle will just ask where we got it and then call Leary to check if it's Alexander's property, and that'll give the whole game away, and then the People in Black will come calling. I think we've got to go back to the home, tell Alexander there's been a misunderstanding and get him to take the book back.'

'He won't talk to us in the home – he has to pretend he's … thingy … catatonic,' Onion insisted. 'And he said to hide it and keep quiet about it.'

'It's not your secret to keep, Onion,' Sive said, grabbing him by the collar of his jacket. 'He has no right to get you in trouble. You're just a kid. *We're all just kids!*'

'I still think it's cool, and I want to read it,' Clíona said. 'I say we meet up behind the store rooms at big break so we can all take a look at it.'

It took a minute for everyone to think it over, but in the end, they all agreed. It meant they could push the problem down the road a bit, and a problem postponed was almost as good as a problem avoided. And it would give them some time to figure out what to do with the time bomb in Onion's schoolbag.

Clíona, however, already knew what she wanted to do with it. She wanted to *read* it. And since she was sitting next to Onion in class, she kept quietly pestering him until he gave in and slid it out of his bag and onto her lap. With great care not be caught by their teacher, Mrs Doyle, she started leafing through the book. Even so, Onion could see her getting more and more excited, and it took her great effort to keep it under control. Clíona was totally geeking out.

CHAPTER EIGHTEEN: WEIRD SCIENCE

By the time the bell rang for big break, she was fit to explode, and the four of them headed towards the relative privacy offered by the section of yard behind the storerooms, where the pupils weren't supposed to go but the teachers rarely bothered to check. They turned the corner to find Tina and the Bang brothers coming in the opposite direction. There was no one else around. They were all out of sight of the teachers.

'Oh, flip,' Onion muttered.

Tina's big blue eyes narrowed in anticipation, her perfect lips spreading in a sly smile. The brothers thumped their fists together. Cliona's face was suddenly very flushed. Sive went to growl something defensive. Onion was about to blurt out that they didn't have any science notebook and Alexander didn't give him anything and who was Alexander anyway? But Dallan saw that his moment had come, and he stepped between the two groups and held his hand up.

'WAIT,' he said to Tina. 'We give up. We're totally in over our heads and we don't want anything to do with this any more. We're ready to tell you everything.'

'You are?' she replied suspiciously.

'Yes,' he said. *'Everything.'*

'Hang on,' she started to say. 'No, wait ... not again.'

'It's the Russians,' he began, talking fast, his voice intense. 'It was always the Russians. They had a secret lab for the spies they were experimenting on, using *alien DNA* and a giant particle accelerator, trying to turn them into *mutant superhumans*. But something went wrong: one of their scientists blasted his own head with an energy beam and his brain grew until he became *as smart as the whole world* and then he stopped thinking because it was, like, too much for a human mind, but before he did, he fired beams from his eyes that switched on all the other mutants' powers and the Russians couldn't control them so they gave them, like, a *special ageing poison* that made them old and forgetful, so they forgot they were superhumans, stopped being a threat, but the aliens – the *aliens* didn't forget ...'

'Oh my God, how do you make him stop?' Tina groaned.

'... The humans had stolen their technology and the aliens went to the Men in – the *People* in Black and demanded that their alien tech be returned, and they wanted all the *mutants* back too because they were part alien now, and the People in Black said sure, but you have to help us find the man with the giant brain, and the aliens said OK, and they used their all-seeing eye stalks and they found the old folks' home full of superhuman mutant ex-spies, *in Ireland*, and the man with the giant brain who was as smart as the whole world was hiding right there in plain sight, right under the People in Black's noses, among the other freaks, pretending to be catapultic –'

'Catatonic,' Clíona corrected him.

'– *catatonic*, and they told the People in Black, the agents of ARSE, who found some kids who were visiting the home, but these black suits couldn't just go following kids on their own because that would look *weird*, so they hired this bully girl and her two thick-plank henchmen to do it for them and – and – and –' Dallan took a deep breath '– and that's how you three chumps ended up working for *aliens*.'

There was a moment's pause before Larry stepped forward and brought a fist down on Dallan's head. Tina swore in exasperation and snarled, 'These losers are such a total waste of time!'

Stepping over the boy who was now lying stunned on the ground, she waved at the brothers and walked off, with the two thugs hurrying to catch up.

But Dr Yury Alexeyev's secret notebook remained safe in Onion's schoolbag.

CHAPTER NINETEEN: A DANGER TO SOCIETY

As soon as school was over, Clíona suggested they take the notebook to her mother, who was a scientist and journalist.

'If Alexander is trying to find someone who can carry on his work, she can help,' Clíona reasoned with them. 'She knows loads of scientists, and this stuff is way beyond what I can get my head around. This guy's, like, an Einstein of microwaves and brain chemistry.'

They were uneasy about it, but the others agreed. Clíona's mum, Vlasta O'Hare, was very encouraging of her daughter's geeky ways, being a complete nerd herself, and let her read, watch and do pretty much what she wanted as long as it wasn't too life-threatening. When Clíona took something seriously, Vlasta let her follow her passions, even if it meant missing school at times. Her daughter did not struggle with schoolwork, and Vlasta believed that children needed to be able to make decisions without adults as often as possible. And it was because of this attitude that the Five O's felt that they could trust Clíona's mum with this weird secret of theirs.

Vlasta was still out at work, but she'd be home that afternoon, and the gang decided to head back to Clíona's house and wait. One factor in this decision was that Clíona had a seriously powerful computer and some really cool games to play while they were waiting. And a tablet. And a laptop. And a phone. And a customised sound system. And some robots that she'd made herself. And her own drinks and snacks cupboard. Clíona could have had the coolest bedroom in all of Ballinlud – if it hadn't been a complete mess all the time, what with the dozens of books, magazines, gadgets and experiments that lay so thick on the floor there was hardly any space to put your feet.

The Five O's were on their way there when they noticed the black SUV gliding along behind them, about fifty metres back. When they stopped, it stopped. When they started walking again, it started rolling again. They stopped again. It stopped. They walked. It rolled. They stopped again and turned to stare at it, but they couldn't see the people in the car because of the dark tinted windows.

'Is anyone totally freaked out right now?' Onion asked. 'Because I am, currently, totally freaked out.'

'I am freaked out also,' Sive said. 'But we can't just keep standing here. What are we going to do?'

'We should run,' Dallan suggested.

'My body doesn't seem to want to move,' Onion said.

Top 5 Things to Do When You're Being Followed by a Big Black Car

1. Run

2. Run

3. Run

4. Breathe, and RUN AGAIN

5. RUN

'I dunno, I think we should go and talk to them?' Clíona offered.

'Then I think you should leave the thinking to us,' Sive replied. 'That's a really daft idea.'

Clíona clearly disagreed, as she started walking towards the car.

'Ah, for pants' sake.' Onion sighed, taking a blast on his inhaler and starting after her.

Watching their friends go, Sive and Dallan had no choice but to follow them. If Clíona was going to get disappeared, the others weren't about to let her go on her own.

As they got closer, the door of the car opened and Elektra McGaffney stepped out, leaning on the car. 'Well, hello,' she said, an amused expression on her face. 'Come for a chat?'

The Five O's looked at each other, with none of them being sure what to say. Clíona took her phone out and took a photo of McGaffney, who struck a pose and smiled, as if being photographed didn't bother her in the slightest.

'Don't worry, I can just wipe that from your phone.' She chuckled. 'But do tell me, what can I do for you, my young friends?

'We want to be left alone,' Sive replied, chewing her gum with a determined expression. 'We don't know what you want, but you and your lot have been hanging around us ever since we started visiting the old folks' home and you have to stop. Just leave us alone.'

'Leave you alone?' the woman in black replied in her Irish American accent. 'Honey, we're here to *protect* you. Oh, look, I understand. I'm guessing you think that A-FoRSE is some shadowy organisation that covers up supernatural goings-on and makes people disappear when they threaten our operations, am I right?'

Trying not to giggle at the name, the Five O's hesitated and then nodded.

'You saw us catch Tara Tunstall in the van and Eoin Macken in the helicopter, and you think we've locked them up in some secret prison, right?'

'Yes!' Onion said. 'Or ... No. Mrs Tunstall was back in the home yesterday.'

'That's right,' McGaffney said, nodding. 'And Mr Macken is back there too, after his little graffiti adventure. That's all we were doing, containing some … difficult situations. You see, we're not the threat, children. *Alexander Yuryev* is. Or, rather, *Dr Yury Alexeyev*. That's his real name, and that's just one of the many truths that man is hiding. He is a very serious danger to society.'

'That's what he says about you!' Onion blurted out.

The other Five O's turned and looked at him, and it was only then he realised the mistake he'd made and slapped his hand to his face. He wished he had some filter between his brain and his mouth. 'Oh, flip,' he groaned.

'So he's spoken to you,' McGaffney said, her eyes narrowing. 'That's *very* interesting. So you know he can walk and talk like any normal person. That's *another* lie he's been living. In fact, you could say his whole life has been one long series of lies. And I think it's time you had a look behind the curtain.

CHAPTER NINETEEN: A DANGER TO SOCIETY

'You see, Dr Alexeyev worked for the Russian government for years, developing technology that could affect people's brains. And then he faked his own death and escaped to Ireland, where we believe he continued his research. Tell me, did he explain how all the residents of this nursing home have suddenly found new energy and enhanced abilities?'

'No,' Onion replied. 'He ... he said it was just old people acting up because they were bored.'

'Oh, *sure* it was,' McGaffney sneered. 'No, Mr O'Brien, this is just more evidence that Alexeyev has been continuing his illegal and dangerous experiments on the innocent and unsuspecting residents of St Brigit's. These poor people could get hurt! All we've been trying to uncover is *how* he's doing it. He has to have a secret lab somewhere, a place equipped with the technology he'd need, and we've been unable to find it.

'And most importantly, we need the plans for that technology, the science behind it, so we can figure out how he's affecting these people's brains before he does some serious harm. It's *vital* we find those plans. They're most likely kept in a … a notebook of some kind. He's too smart to leave records on any kind of computer. If we could find that notebook, we could expose him and show the world what kind of brain-altering monster he really is.

'And I hate to say it, but we can't do it alone. He's spent his whole life learning how to avoid law enforcers. We need help. And I think you could help us. So what do you say, children? Will you help us bring down this criminal mastermind before he can spring his plans on the world?'

The Five O's looked at one another, unspoken agreement passing between them.

'Yeah, OK,' Onion said. 'We'll do it.'

CHAPTER TWENTY:
—
UNDER NEW
MANAGEMENT

The Five O's had no intention of helping Elektra McGaffney and the agents of A-FoRSE, but they figured she might leave them alone if she thought they were. She gave them a number to call if they found out any information about Alexeyev's notes and then drove off.

She had made a good point, though. While Alexander had denied it, he was definitely having some kind of effect on the residents in the nursing home. And if he did have some secret lab, and he was messing with their brains, it *could* be dangerous.

Even so, the Five O's were still more suspicious of the People in Black than the Russian scientist.

Their loyalty to Alexander wasn't based on anything solid; there was no reason to believe McGaffney was a bigger liar than he was, except the Five O's were all outcasts in one way or another, a gang of kids who didn't fit in very well with the others in their school or neighbourhood, and instinctively, they knew Alexander was the same, someone who had never fit in.

It took one to know one.

Onion and the others didn't want to wait around until Clíona's mum got home, in case the People in Black were still spying on them somehow, realised what they were doing and caught them with the notebook. They had to stay on the move, and while they did, they had to work out how to shake off the PIB long enough for Clíona's mum to take the notebook to someone who could help.

'Whatever happens, it's really important that we don't go anywhere near St Brigit's,' Onion said firmly. 'ARSE will have their eyes all over that place.'

It was at that moment that Grandad pulled up in the car and leaned out the window. 'Where have you kids been?' he called out. 'Give up acting the maggot and hop in. Mary wants you down in St Brigit's as soon as possible. Sive, Dallan, Clíona, we've already checked it with your parents. C'mon now, let's get the show on the road ... hahahahaha!' Grandad cackled and waved them into the car.

There was no arguing with him, so they reluctantly climbed in. He was listening to a phone-in show on the radio, had it up good and loud, and once the children were in the car, he paid no more attention to them. The people on the radio were talking about the mysterious blackouts in South Dublin, and what could be causing them.

'I was thinking about that,' Clíona whispered to the others, including Onion, who had to lean in from the front seat. 'The things I was reading about in the notebook were using microwaves, but really unusual, powerful ones. I think they'd take a lot of power – like, *serious* amounts. Have you noticed that there was a power cut every time one of the old folk came out and did something mad?'

Actually, they hadn't, but now that she mentioned it, it seemed obvious to them, so they all nodded.

'I think Alexander's doing something that's pulling loads of power down from the grid every time, and it's crashing the network somehow,' she said. 'Like blowing a fuse in your house. That means it's got to be a pretty big machine. He'd need space for it. And wherever Alexander's lab is, it has to be somewhere close by or he wouldn't be able to sneak away to it without being missed. We should see if we can get him alone and talk to him while we're there. If he won't tell us what he's up to, then we need to try and find his lab.'

'But the PIB *own* the nursing home now,' Dallan pointed out. 'Onion said they were putting cameras up all over the place. If they can't find the lab, what chance have we got?'

'Maybe we can persuade Alexander to show us, since we're helping him. He owes us that much, doesn't he?' Clíona said. She tended to think everyone was as open-minded and well-meaning as she was.

'And if he doesn't show us?' Onion asked. 'I don't think we should be helping him if he really is doing dangerous experiments.'

'Y'know, my dad's company built that place. He probably still has the plans in his office at the yard,' Sive said. She was less innocent than Clíona. 'Maybe we could sneak a peek at them and see if there are any secret spaces?'

'How would Leary not know if there was a secret room in his own building?' Onion asked. 'I mean, he runs the place. OK, he's a cheap, greedy sod, but he's not a complete idiot.'

'He's got a guy who's supposed to be stuck in a wheelchair who goes missing on a regular basis,' Dallan pointed out. 'And a bunch of others who've just walked out of the place, done some mad stuff and been chased by the guards all around town. I don't think he's the most observant fella we've ever met. Or he just doesn't *care* what's going on, unless he can make some money out of it.'

'OK, then, let's search the place when we get there, and find this secret lab, and see what Alexander's really been up to,' Onion said. 'If we don't have any luck, we can do like Sive says and check those plans.'

And so, they had the beginnings of a plan. It was a bit risky, and not very well thought out, but it was a start.

It went wrong almost immediately.

CHAPTER TWENTY: UNDER NEW MANAGEMENT

'In ye go – sorry I can't join ye, but I have the paper to get.' Grandad winked at Onion as he laughed and drove off.

They saw the black SUV and the van parked at the top of the driveway. They spotted Elektra McGaffney in Leary's office as they came in and walked past the open door.

And though Granny was already set up for the dancing, nobody was going to be strutting any disco moves. Ursula was as slow and placid as she'd been the first day, as were all the others. Derek showed up not long after the other four and tried to hide his disappointment that there'd be no pulse-pounding dance experience today. They were back to '*One*, two, three, *one*, two, three …'

It was easy to see why there were no more strange goings-on in the home. There were now cameras in every room. Black-suited figures wandered up and down the hallways. Elektra McGaffney sat in on the dance class, smiling and complimenting the old folk on their practice and generally making everyone uneasy. Nobody was going to try anything out of the ordinary while the agents of A-FoRSE were all over the place.

Alexander was back in his wheelchair in the dining room, looking zoned out, with a tall, muscular agent sitting next to him reading a magazine. Clíona sat down next to him and made a bit of small talk, but got no reaction at all from him.

Danilo and the rest of the staff seemed a bit freaked out and kept talking too loudly and dropping things. They weren't happy to have their residents being bothered by these overbearing, black-suited strangers. Unlike Leary, they did care about these people.

When the dance class was over, McGaffney walked Granny and the Five O's to the front door and thanked them for their time.

'I don't think we'll be needing any more dance classes,' she added. 'It's too much to ask of you, and to be frank, I think it's a strain on these poor dears. This will be the last session. We are grateful for your efforts, and you're welcome to keep in touch.' She stared at Onion as she said this. 'But now that the home is under new ownership, we're going to be making a lot of changes around here.'

'Oh, that's a shame!' Granny sighed. 'I thought we were making great progress. They really seemed to be enjoying it. Are you sure you won't change your mind?'

'I don't change my mind,' McGaffney told her.

And that was that. McGaffney gave Onion and the others a knowing wink, waved to Granny, stepped back inside and closed the door. Onion was left with the distinct impression that, if Elektra McGaffney had her way, Alexander would never leave that building again.

CHAPTER TWENTY-ONE:
—
FLOOR PLAN

Sive's dad ran a construction company, and years before, the company had knocked down a ruined old farmhouse that dated all the way back to when Ballinlud was just a village near Dublin. Once the site was cleared, they'd built what was now St Brigit's of the Weeping Wound. Sive's dad kept the plans for every building he'd constructed, and Sive knew where those plans were stored.

Unfortunately, they were kept in her dad's office in the builder's yard, and Sive didn't want her parents knowing what they were mixed up in, so that meant if they wanted to look at the plans, the

Five O's would have to, well … sneak into the office. Derek was steaming because of the way the PIB had thrown them out, and he was all up for joining the others in finding the lab before the A-FoRSE agents could and sticking it to the Man, though he insisted he still wasn't in the Five O's' stupid gang.

They met on the green after dinner and homework, as it was starting to get dark, and set off for the yard. Clíona had a small backpack with

her, as she often did for her odds and ends. She was carrying the notebook in it, as nobody could agree on a safe place to leave it unattended.

The builder's yard was in a small business park near the far end of the Valley, closer to the nursing home than it was to Sive's house. It closed at five, after all the builders had finished on their sites and brought the equipment back to the yard, but the two-metre-high steel gates were made to keep the trucks

and equipment in, not keep kids out. Climbing over wasn't too hard if you had someone to give you a boost up or to reach down and help pull you up.

The office building was at the back of the yard, past the trucks and diggers and cement mixers and other heavy machinery. Sive told them to wait for a minute and headed around the back. Derek peered at the lock on the ever-so-solid front door, chewed his lip and then nodded confidently to himself. 'This shouldn't take too long.' He pulled a wire coat-hanger from the back of his trousers and started twisting the hook into a straighter shape. Then he stuck the end into the lock and began wiggling it around. With his face in close to the lock, he grimaced, jiggling the wire as if he was trying to catch it on something, then trying to twist something, then trying to force it in. He leaned his head hard on the door, just over the handle, both hands gripping the end of the coat-hanger ... when the door suddenly opened and he went hurtling inside, yelping in fright, and landed with a thud on the floor. Sive was standing there, holding the door open. 'They always leave the toilet window open round the back,' she said. 'You only had towait, Derek.'

Derek, who had landed square on his nose on the heavy-duty carpet, grunted in reply. He was bleeding from both nostrils and had a pink carpet burn on his nose. Pretending this was no big deal, he waved the others in as if this had been his plan all along.

They'd all brought torches, and they switched them on, rather than turning on the lights in the gloomy hallway. Sive led them past a row of doors and up a set of stairs. She'd told them that the old sets of plans were in a storeroom on the first floor.

Top 5 Things You Need If You're Going to Break into a Place

1. Lock-pick

2. Small human to slide in through tiny gaps, like a partly opened window

3. Non-squeaky shoes

4. Fresh underpants in case you poo yourself

5. A good lawyer

Creeping upstairs, they reached the top and peered cautiously around. Sive made a series of hand gestures to communicate what they had to do, as if they were a squad of soldiers on patrol in enemy territory. They needed the key to the storeroom, which was in her dad's office, but she needed the other four to go to different windows to keep watch in case someone showed up.

Onion was to be stationed by the window at the end of the hallway. He'd only just got there when he peered down into the alley on one side of the building and frowned. 'Hey, Sive?' he whispered. 'Isn't that your dad's car –?'

'Sive?' They all nearly jumped out of their skins as her father walked out of his office. 'What are you doing here, love? How'd you get in? I thought I'd locked the door.'

CHAPTER TWENTY-ONE: FLOOR PLAN

Mick O'Connor was a wide man with a rough face, messy dark blond hair, hefty shoulders and builder's arms. He mostly just managed construction projects these days, but he still had the look about him of a man who'd grown up on building sites.

'I – we –' Sive stuttered, going very pale.

'Sorry to bother you, Mr O'Connor –' Dallan began.

'Mick, please. I'm always saying you don't have to call me "Mr O'Connor", Dallan.'

'Well, Mick,' Dallan began again, 'we were supposed to be helping out down in the nursing home this evening, but we came all the way down and the new owners said they didn't want our help – they were pretty mean about it, actually – and she won't admit this because you know how tough she likes to be, y'see, but Sive was a bit upset because they're not being very nice to those old folks, that Leary fella especially, and she didn't know what to do about it, so ... so ...'

'So, she came looking for her dad,' Mick said, giving his daughter an understanding smile. 'Poor pet. Yeah, he's a right piece of work, that guy Leary. Never liked him.'

Sive glanced at Dallan, sniffed loudly and threw her arms around her dad in a big hug. He hugged her back and ruffled her spiky hair.

'Here, didn't *you* build that nursing home?' Onion spoke up.

'We did indeed. One of our first big projects.'

'Could we have a look at the plans?' Clíona asked. 'I *love* building plans.'

This was a completely reasonable question coming from Clíona, and Mick considered it for a moment and then shrugged. Like many people who loved their work, he always assumed other people would love it too. 'I suppose, why not? They're just down here.'

He took them to the storeroom and unlocked the door, which opened into a small space filled with sets of shelves full of cubbyholes. He found the rolled-up architect's plans for St Brigit's and spread the big sheets out on a table. There were very precise drawings of the front, back and sides of the building and the layouts of the two floors, with lots of measurements and notes on the types of materials.

'This was a farmhouse before, wasn't it?' Derek asked.

'Yeah, though it's all gone now,' Mick told him. He was warming to his subject, what with the kids taking such an interest. 'Big old place it was. Massive septic tank out the back.'

'What's that?' Dallan said.

'It's a tank where all your poo and pee from your toilet goes if you're not connected to the pipes in a town,' Mick told him. 'You have to pump it out when it's full.'

'Ew!' Dallan winced.

'Buildings have got to have toilets, lad. You'd be pretty stuck without one, wouldn't yeh? Anyway, the property's on the town sewage system now, so we filled that in. There was a cellar too. The farmer was loaded, and he loved his wine. Had a cellar dug just for storing it.'

Mick pointed at the spot, and Onion looked at the sheet, then around at the others. 'That's funny – it's not in the building,' he said. 'It looks like it's out in the yard at the side. I've been out there. There's no door into a cellar there.'

'No, we walled it up,' Mick said. 'The client didn't want to spend any more money fixing it up. It's still there, though, with good stone walls and solid beams for the ceiling, in case they ever want to dig it out and make some extra storage space.'

CHAPTER TWENTY-ONE: FLOOR PLAN

Onion gazed at the spot again. According to the plans, the steps to the cellar were right under the shed in the yard where he'd hidden in the wheelie bin – where Alexander had brought him for their secret night-time rendezvous. There had to be a hidden entrance somewhere in the shed.

They'd found the Russian scientist's secret laboratory.

CHAPTER TWENTY-TWO:
THE SECRET
LABORATORY

The Five O's pretended to Sive's dad that they were going to walk home and maybe hang out on the green for a while. It was getting dark now, but still wasn't that late. Instead, they made their way down the Valley and through the woods to the wall of the nursing home. Getting close to the wall, they were careful to be quiet, in case any of the agents were on watch out in the grounds.

Onion had come this way before, so he climbed the tree against the wall first to look over into the small yard where the bins were kept. There was no

CHAPTER TWENTY-TWO: THE SECRET LABORATORY

sign of a guard; he clambered over and the others followed. Looking around, they could see no sign of a hidden hatch down into the cellar, which made sense, as it would have to be a *hidden* hatch. Onion tried the door of the shed and found it unlocked. Stepping inside, he switched on his torch and peered around.

At first glance, it looked like a typical gardening shed, with tools on hooks or standing against the walls and a lawnmower, strimmer and hedge trimmer pushed in to one corner. There were plant pots and bags of compost and lawn feed. It all looked very ordinary. But Onion *knew* there was a room underneath this floor, and the more he stared at the floorboards, the more he started to see.

At one spot, the joints in the floorboards lined up so that there was a square seam, about a metre by a metre. There was a hole near one edge. He stuck his finger into the hole and pulled, and the whole piece of floor came up. Here was their secret hatch. A ladder led down into a passageway. Light was coming from further in. Onion looked at the others and shivered with nerves and excitement.

He took a blast of his inhaler, put one foot on the ladder, slipped and tumbled down through the hole with a loud squeal, banging his head and knocking his glasses off as he went.

The other Five O's exchanged glances, shook their heads and followed their friend down the ladder at a more sensible pace. They found themselves in a short stretch of passageway with stone walls and a stone roof supported by thick wooden beams. At the end of the passageway was a well-lit room with a tall chair sitting in the middle of it and pieces of computer equipment and other machinery positioned around it. The chair looked like a cross between some kind of medieval torture device and the command chair from a spaceship in *Star Trek*. It had wires and cables trailing from it to the computers and a complicated helmet attached to an arm on the top.

The strange piece of technology had grabbed their attention as soon as they'd entered the room, so it took another couple of seconds to realise they weren't alone. Standing off to one side was Alexander Yuryev, up and out of his wheelchair ... and Elektra McGaffney. One of McGaffney's agents was standing on the other side of the room, a hulking guy with slicked-back hair, trying to work something on the machine.

'I *knew* it!' she exclaimed as she saw the kids. 'I *knew* you were mixed up in this somehow! So much for being my little snitches, eh? You were

Alexander's loyal chumps all along.' She saw the expressions on their faces. 'Oh, I get it. You *just found this place*, didn't you? You worked it out somehow – thought you were being clever? Did you really think you'd find this lab before we did?'

'Sort of, yes,' Onion admitted, feeling bitterly disappointed.

'Well, maybe you can still be useful,' she said. 'Alexander's not playing ball. He won't tell us how to work the machine, and I don't want to start taking it apart without the instructions. We've searched every inch of this lab and the whole nursing home and can't find any sign of his notes.'

She stepped closer to Onion and leaned in, so there were only centimetres between their faces. It was as if she could smell that he was the weak link when it came to keeping a secret. 'I don't suppose *you* know where his notebook is?'

Onion's wonky eye started moving, and he did his best to stop it. It swivelled around a bit, and McGaffney's gaze followed its twitches with interest.

'You could be in so much trouble,' she said in a stern voice. 'Terrible, *terrible* trouble.'

The stupid, rebellious eye was about to pivot round and point at Clíona's backpack, when Onion clenched his eyes shut, shaking his head.

McGaffney aimed her stare at each of the kids in turn, the intensity of it threatening to break their nerve and make them talk. 'Perhaps you've hidden it,' she said hoarsely. 'Or … perhaps one of you has it on you right now?'

'Don't be a fool,' Alexander rasped. 'They're not complete idiots! They'd never be that stupid to bring the notebook here.'

Onion opened his eyes. He'd broken into a sweat and gone very pale.

'You didn't, did you?' Alexander said, his mouth dropping open. 'Oh my God, you *did*! You brought the notebook *here*?' There was a moment of electrical tension as everything seemed to hang motionless, and then the Russian took a deep breath and bellowed: '*Run*, you fools! Get

out of here and run for your lives! **RUN!'**

McGaffney seized Clíona and pulled the bag off her back. Clíona was knocked to the floor, but Derek slammed his shoulder into the woman in black, snatching the pack from her hand as she stumbled and hit her head against the wall. He tossed the bag to Onion and shouted at him to run, keeping himself between McGaffney, her agent and the Five O's. Onion took the bag and sprinted off up the passageway, with Sive and Dallan close behind him. Then Derek turned and followed them.

'Stay here – **WATCH THEM!'** McGaffney snarled at her agent, pointing at Alexander and Clíona. Then she rushed off after the four remaining Five O's, already on the phone to call in the rest of her A-FoRSE team.

Alexander helped Clíona up, glanced at the time on his chunky old digital watch and turned to the agent who'd been left to guard them. 'Sir, please stand away from the machine,' he said. 'I'd rather you didn't touch it.'

'What – this machine?' the agent said, putting his hand on the chair, a nasty smirk on his face. 'Why, what you going to do about it?'

Alexander pressed a button on his watch and the agent suddenly went as stiff as a board as a massive electrical jolt ran through his body. He toppled over, groaning, and the Russian quickly tied him up with a couple of spare cables. '*That's* what I'm going to do about it,' he replied.

'**The notebook!**' Clíona cried. 'We have to stop them getting the notebook.'

'Don't worry about the notebook, my dear,' Alexander said. 'We have work to do and not much time to do it. I need your help.' He sat down in the chair and pulled the helmet down over his head. 'My ... my mind has been fading as I get older. Everything I know is being lost, bit by bit. I need to boost my brain with this machine, but the effect is only ever temporary. I don't have much time left. Eventually, it will stop working altogether, and only my research notes will remain. Before that happens, we have things to do.'

Fitting the helmet in place, he noted the time on his watch, then used a permanent marker to write another time on his wrist. 'That is my deadline, like Cinderella going to the ball and having to be home by midnight,'

he said. 'I have two hours before the effect wears off and my mind begins to go dull again. Now stand back, please.'

He reached over to a big green button on the bank of computers beside him and pressed it.

CHAPTER TWENTY-TWO: THE SECRET LABORATORY

Lights went on in the helmet, and the whole room started to hum. The room's lights flickered and Clíona could smell electricity in the air as the machine drained the power grid. A red light in the shape of a crosshairs appeared in the middle of Alexander's forehead and then he grunted and his head jolted back.

Everything powered down, and he blinked and then smiled at Clíona. 'That's better, I have my full faculties once more,' he said. 'And the machine's batteries are charged up too.'

'That's amazing,' she said. 'But what are we going to do now?'

'My dear,' he said, laughing, 'we're only getting started.'

CHAPTER TWENTY-THREE: HUNTED

Onion's breathing was strained as he ran. He kept his torch off so that it would be harder for the People in Black to see him, even though it meant that it was harder to see where he was going. Well, he thought, here I am running through the woods again.

Derek, Dallan and Sive were close behind him. They were all better runners and would have overtaken him if the path was wide enough and they could actually see where it was. As it was, he was only keeping up this pace out of pure terror and adrenaline. Even if the agents couldn't see him or hear his footsteps, they could probably track his wheezing through the darkness. He wondered what had happened to Clíona.

The beams of torches stabbed the darkness behind them, and the agents of A-FoRSE called out to each other, combing the woods for their quarry. They were fit and hard and the kids wouldn't be able to outrun them for long. The four Five O's needed somewhere to hide.

Off to his left, Onion saw the lights of the houses nearby cut out and go dark. Another power outage. Had the People in Black figured out how to use Alexander's machine? What were they doing with it? He hadn't realised just how dark it could be among the trees without the glow from the houses and streetlights fifty or sixty metres away. He couldn't see a thing. He had to slow down and switch on his torch, picking out the path in front of him. Behind him, he could hear more shouts as the agents saw his torchlight.

He turned off the torch again as the Five O's came out of the trees, following the track along the

stream, running as hard as they could along the length of the Valley, until they came to the low tunnel where the Big Leak ran under the road at the end. Onion ducked into the gloom of the tunnel, barely able to breathe, and took another blast of his inhaler. The others piled in around him, and they hid there, catching their breath, as they saw the torches come out of the trees at the other end of the Valley. The agents clearly thought they were still in the woods.

Somewhere overhead, the Five O's heard the hushed engines of the black helicopter, searching from above.

CHAPTER TWENTY-THREE: HUNTED

'Where are we going to go?' Dallan asked. 'We can't stay here – they'll find us. Even if we go back home, they'll find us. What are we going to do?'

'Let's ... let's just stay ahead of them until we come up with a plan,' Derek panted. 'We need somewhere safer to hide until the heat dies down. Give us a bit of time to think.'

'Where, though?' Onion wheezed. 'Where can we go?'

'The yard. We should head for Dad's yard,' Sive said. 'It's only a few minutes from here.'

Nobody had any better ideas, so they waited a while longer, getting their breath back, and watched the searchers gradually get closer as they made their way in a line across the Valley, the beams of the torches waving from right to left like radar. Finally, the Five O's couldn't wait any longer, and they crawled along beside the stream, through the tunnel to the other side of the road and out onto the bit of waste ground that backed onto the high wall of the business park. From there, it was only a few hundred metres' run to the builder's yard.

They never even got close. A garda car pulled up on the road above them and the Ferg stepped out. He hadn't seen them yet. The stocky guard was wearing a black suit now too. Perhaps he was applying to join A-FoRSE.

'Are those suits infectious or what?' Derek hissed. 'They're spreading like a skin disease.'

Judge was in her normal uniform, sitting behind the wheel, and she looked past her partner and pointed. 'There! Over there!'

No sooner had she said it than the black SUV screeched to a halt behind their car and two agents leaped out. They scrambled down the bank and were almost on top of the kids when a shrill whistle stopped them in their tracks. The two men looked up in time to see a dark shape leap off the bank and land on them, slamming them to the ground. Ursula Stockton stood, a little shaken but not stirred, and elbowed one of the men in the jaw as he started to get up, before kicking him in the chest and bringing her knee up into the side of his head. He collapsed to the ground.

The other guy hesitated before hitting the old woman, and she took full advantage of it by kicking him between the legs, getting her hands around his headand slamming his face down on her knee.

He groaned and crumpled into a heap. The two men were down, but the Ferg and Garda Judge were coming now too, with more agents behind them.

Everything was suddenly blanketed in a blinding light. From above, a searchlight shone down and they could hear the helicopter, feel the wind from its powerful rotors.

Ursula turned to the Five O's, a little out of breath, and pointed to the wall. 'On you go, now,' she said. 'Eoin's waiting for you.'

They hurried down along the wall that bordered the nursing home and found Eoin, the graffiti artist, had hijacked another cherry-picker. It was on the other side of the wall, and he'd lowered the platform down to where the kids could reach it. He waved them on, and they climbed aboard as he took the controls again.

The guards and the agents watched helplessly as the Five O's were lifted up out of reach and over the wall, which was too high for the adults to climb. The pursuers immediately split up, some running for the cars, others looking for a point where they could get over the wall.

'**Keep going!**' Eoin told them as he lowered the platform down to the other side and they jumped out. 'Head down the main road. Try and keep out of sight!'

The kids started running again. The light from the helicopter followed them, the bright searchlight tracking their movement, the crew reporting the kids' position to the agents on the ground. They were getting tired and didn't know how they could get out of this. The garda car swerved around a corner, with the black SUV right behind it. Judge saw the kids and suddenly did a handbrake turn, swinging her car sideways on the road and blocking the other car. Her window was open, so the kids heard the Ferg shout at his partner: 'Bridie, what the flip are you doing, woman?'

'I've had it with being told what to do by these jumped-up, pathetic James Bond wannabes, Fergus!' Judge snapped.

'But they're in charge, Bridie! The sarge says we have to do what they say! And I only just got the suit!'

'Stuff them *and* their bleedin' suits,' Judge replied. Calling over to the Five O's, she added, 'You lot, get outta here! Go home and stay out of trouble!'

With the road blocked, the A-FoRSE agents had to get out of their car and follow on foot. But they were still fit and fast and dead set on catching their prey. The Five O's started running again, and though they were trying their best, the man and two women behind them were seconds away from running them down.

'GIVE US THAT NOTEBOOK!' one of them yelled. 'Just give us the book and this will all be over! Come on, kids, there's nowhere to go. Give it up!'

One of them grabbed Dallan, and Derek turned back to try and help and was tackled to the ground by another agent. The third was still coming and he'd be on Onion in moments. It was then that they all heard the growl of a motorbike engine, which rose to a roar as a figure raced out from behind a building. It was Mrs Tunstall, back on Austin Leary's beloved motorcycle.

The helicopter's light blazed over her as she flicked the back wheel in a skid that took the legs out from under the agent and then pulled up alongside Onion, dragging him up onto the saddle behind her. 'Got that notebook?' she asked.

CHAPTER TWENTY-THREE: HUNTED

Onion nodded, too out of breath to speak, holding up the backpack.

'Hold on tight, Onion, love,' she said. 'It's time to burn some rubber.'

Revving the engine, she spun the bike around, the back tyre leaving a curving black streak on the concrete, and then she tore out of the business park at a speed that had a petrified Onion O'Brien aching for a toilet.

CHAPTER TWENTY-FOUR:
—
THE END OF THE LINE

Mrs Tunstall led the A-FoRSE vehicles a winding chase through the suburban maze of Ballinlud. The power had come back on, so the area had lit back up. And no matter what she did to evade the vehicles on the ground, the helicopter was always able to find her from above. Onion held on for dear life as she did skid-turns, wove in among parked cars, rode through people's gardens and zigzagged through traffic, narrowly missing slamming into the cars around her. He screamed most of the way. Car and motorbike chases looked cool on film, but they were terrifying in real life.

CHAPTER TWENTY-FOUR: THE END OF THE LINE

Mrs Tunstall's course took her in a loop, and they were heading back towards the Valley along a narrow residential road lined with parked cars on either side, when the A-FoRSE van blocked the road in front of them. The agents jumped out, ready to grab the bike if the old lady hooligan rider tried to get past on the paths either side. Behind the bike, the SUV closed off their retreat; they were trapped between the agents either end and the lines of parked cars on either side. Mrs Tunstall looked one way, then the other, and took a deep breath.

'For a moment there, I thought we were in trouble,' she said.

'What?' Onion whimpered.

'Hang on,' she added.

'I've been hanging on the whole time!' Onion wailed. 'I can't hang on any more than I was hanging on already!'

The motorbike let out a loud snarl, Mrs Tunstall kicked it into a wheelie and then bounced it up onto the bonnet of the car parked beside her. Then she rode it up on the roof and down the back, hopping onto the bonnet of the next car, jolting Onion to his bones. As he heard the crunch of breaking glass beneath their wheels, he winced, clenched his eyes shut and tried not to think of the damage they were doing. They rode down the line of five parked cars, past the reaching hands of the agents and dropped down onto the road again, pulling away at speed, the back tyre screeching.

He opened his eyes and looked up, squinting when he saw a strange orange glow in the dark sky. 'What's that?' he asked.

But he could already tell; it was a fire, a big one. **'That's *St Brigit's*!'** Mrs Tunstall said, a tremor in her voice. 'The nursing home's on fire!'

Onion was going to tell her that they couldn't go back there, that the whole point was that they were trying to *get away* from there, but how could he tell her to ignore what was happening to her friends? How could she turn her back when her home was on fire? As they got closer, however, it was clear that, though the fire alarm was going off, the building itself wasn't on fire. They rode up the driveway and stopped.

Everyone who could had come out of the building to look, and staff were busy helping those who couldn't move themselves to a safe distance. Austin Leary wasn't helping; he was just standing there with his niece, Tina Dalton, and the twin brothers. All of them were scowling at the blaze. Leary let out a squeal and started sobbing when he looked round and saw the state of his battered and buckled motorbike.

The shed was on fire, ferocious flames rising into the air, billowing smoke. It wasn't just the shed, of course, it was the *laboratory* beneath it. All of Alexander's equipment, his miraculous machine ... all destroyed. Fire engines were pulling up at the gates, but they would be far too late to save the lab. The first lot of firefighters began pulling hoses from their truck.

Onion looked frantically around until he saw Clíona and Alexander standing nearby. They too were staring at the flames. An agent with slicked-back hair was lying on the ground at their feet, his wrists and ankles tied up with cables. Clíona appeared sad, but Alexander was smiling.

Onion hurried over to them. 'What happened?' he demanded. 'What's going on?'

'I couldn't let them have my machine,' Alexander told him. 'Your gang and my friends from the home helped keep McGaffney's people away just long enough for me to destroy everything. They would have taken my work from me and used it to brainwash people, to hurt people. I couldn't allow that.'

The People in Black were pulling into the small car park in the van and the SUV. Elektra McGaffney leaped out of the SUV and hurried towards Alexander. Behind her, Onion could see Derek, Sive and Dallan getting out of the van.

'But it could have helped people too!' Clíona said. 'Look what it did for the people here. Look how it kept your own brain working. What are you going to do now?'

'It's too late for me, my dear,' Alexander said with a sad smile. 'There isn't much left in me. But

I have no regrets – I've enjoyed my life, and I got to see my machine working at last.'

'We have your notes,' Onion said, still trying to catch his breath. 'Couldn't we pass them on to someone else? Someone you trust?'

'Ah, yes, the notes,' he replied, taking the book from Onion. 'I'm afraid I don't trust *anyone* any more.'

McGaffney was striding up to them, a furious expression on her face. Alexander took one last look at his notebook ... and then went to throw it in the fire.

'What the hell –?' Onion exclaimed.

'NOOOO!' McGaffney screamed, clawed hands reaching out. 'What are you doing? **WHAT ARE YOU DOING?'**

'I will make a deal with you, Elektra,' Alexander said, holding the notebook back. With his free hand, he took a tablet from the pocket of his suit jacket. 'I have just over an hour before the effects of the machine wear off and my mind starts to fade again. Without my machine, it will be for the last time. I didn't have much left in me anyway. And I won't remember any of my research soon. There will only be my notes left. But if you promise to look after my friends in the nursing home, you can have the notebook. You won't have my machine, but I can share some of my knowledge.'

'Yes,' she said desperately. '*Whatever you want*, you can have it! Just name your price.'

'Extensive work needs to be done the nursing home. I have *detailed plans*.'

'Yes, yes, anything you want!' she gasped, throwing her hands in the air.

'Extensive work.'

'Can we just get it over with?'

'The contract is all set up here – you just have to approve it,' he said, handing over the tablet. 'You are to hand ownership of the home over to Danilo, who will manage things from now on. Austin Leary is fired with immediate effect. The staff are to get pay rises, the building is to be upgraded and there will be better food for the residents and all the therapy and activities they need – and *you* will pay for *all of it*.'

'All right, all right, but we get you too! No more avoiding us, Alexeyev, no more trying to hide or escape.'

'No, no, I'm all yours,' he said. 'I'll come quietly.'

McGaffney took the tablet, cast her eyes over it impatiently, then pressed her finger on the screen, which read her fingerprint and sealed the contract. 'There ... *done*. It's done. That will all be taken care of.'

'Thank you,' he said.

CHAPTER TWENTY-FOUR: THE END OF THE LINE

He turned to the Five O's. Derek, Sive and Dallan were now standing with Onion. Clíona was standing slightly apart, and she was crying. Alexander put a hand on her shoulder and gave it a squeeze. 'Don't be sad for me, my dear,' he said. 'I've lived a very full life and I've ensured a better future for my friends. I've helped make them happier. I don't think any of us can ask for more than that, can we?'

Something occurred to him, and he held up a finger. 'Oh, and one more thing. I don't think I'll be needing this old thing any more. I'd like you to have it.' He took off his chunky digital watch and handed to her. 'I know you like taking stuff apart to find out how it works,' he added. He clasped his hands around hers as she took the watch. 'This was the first thing *I* ever took apart, when I was a child, and I've kept it ever since. It's yours now.'

'That's enough with the goodbyes,' McGaffney said impatiently, holding her hand out. 'We need to go. We've attracted too much attention already. Time to hold up your end of the deal.'

'Ready when you are, Agent McGaffney,' he said. He handed her the notebook and gave a last wave to the Five O's, who waved back.

Then he turned and walked with the woman in the black suit, past the rushing firefighters and the staff and residents of the nursing home, to the black van that waited with its doors open. He got in, the doors closed and that was the last the Five O's ever saw of Alexander Yuryev, also known as Dr Yury Alexeyev.

CHAPTER TWENTY-FIVE:
—
ONE LAST THING

Three months later, the four core members of the Five O's were back visiting the residents of St Brigit's of the Weeping Wound. But the nursing home would have been barely recognisable to anyone who'd visited months before.

Elektra McGaffney had kept her word, and Alexander's plans for the place had been followed to the letter. The building had been completely renovated. Sive's dad's company had done most of the construction, though all sorts of experts had been brought in to complete the work.

The place had everything its residents could ask for, including landscaped gardens and a generously equipped games room, complete with a snooker table. There was a cinema, physical therapy rooms, a hair and beauty suite, a chapel, a library and even a small swimming pool. And it was no longer called St Brigit's of the Weeping Wound. Now, it was the Yuryev Home of Long Lives. An oil painting hung over the fireplace in the living room. It showed Alexander standing with the other residents. Commissioned as part of the work on the building, it even featured Granny and the Five O's standing in the background.

A fire burned brightly in the hearth that day, and the room buzzed with activity. Granny and Derek were leading dance lessons again. Dallan was chatting to some of the ladies, who were giving him advice about girls. Sive was playing *Kill-Death-Zombie-Cannons* with Francie O'Halloran, which he found helped him wonderfully with his memory. Even Grandad was there, down the hall, where he was finishing painting Ursula's bedroom.

Onion was sitting at a table with Clíona and Pixel Pat. Clíona had taken Alexander's old watch apart again. She did this every couple of weeks, because the first time she'd done it, she'd found components in there that didn't make any sense.

'I can't believe he handed his notebook over like that, after everything we did to try and stop McGaffney from getting it,' Onion grumbled as he watched her. 'What about all that stuff he said about the People in Black using the machine to do bad stuff?'

'I suppose there was nothing else he could do,' Sive said as she got her character to duck under a low-flying saw blade. 'Everything was against him. And you heard what he said. His mind was failing. He probably figured he had no choice. And he did make sure the old folk would be looked after.'

'Still,' Onion said sullenly, 'it just feels like ... like ... like the *good guys lost*, y'know? McGaffney got what she wanted, Alexander disappeared ... It's just not fair.'

Clíona looked up at him. 'McGaffney didn't get anything.'

'What do you mean?' Onion asked. Sive paused the game and Dallan looked up from his conversation.

'There's nothing valuable in the notebook,' Clíona replied. 'It was a decoy. It was *always* a decoy because people were always trying to steal Alexander's plans. The information in it looks really important, but if you try to make the machine, the plans will lead you round in circles. The notebook was there to attract everyone's attention. It was *made to be stolen*.'

CHAPTER TWENTY-FIVE: ONE LAST THING

'You mean we did ... all of that,' Onion waved his hand around generally to refer to the chaos of their dramatic chase, 'for absolutely nothing? It was a complete waste of time?'

'Not for nothing,' Clíona said. 'Or, eh ... I mean, yes and no. You did it so that it *would* be a complete waste of time – for McGaffney and her goons. It gave Alexander a chance to destroy the lab and his machine, so ARSE wouldn't get their hands on it. And even *he* can't remember most of his research any more.'

'Why are you only telling us this now?' Dallan asked, coming over.

'He made me promise to keep it a secret until the home was rebuilt,' she replied. 'He wouldn't say why.'

'You kept that from us for *three months*?' Onion exclaimed.

'I made a promise,' she said, shrugging. 'But I thought ... I dunno ... that I'd see him again. I thought he'd find a way around McGaffney. I guess he didn't.'

'See?' Onion said. 'It *does* feel like we lost.'

Clíona grunted in exasperation as she returned her concentration to her work. She'd seen the Russian use his chunky watch to switch on his machine, but it seemed to be more than just a remote control. She couldn't figure out what some of the circuitry was for or how it worked. She had decided to ask Pixel to look at it, only to find that he was just as baffled.

'Can't help you, love,' he said. 'It's beyond me. Some of this new tech stuff just goes over my head.'

It was at that moment, as Clíona sighed and clicked the watch's cover back into place, that a thin beam shot out of the screen and right over Pixel's head. The beam was pulsing slightly. Onion opened his mouth to ask a question, then shut it again as Clíona held up her hand. 'It's never done this before,' she said. 'It's like it's reacting to something. This is the first time we've been back in the building since they did all the work on it. Maybe there's something in here it's picking up on?'

'You mean like – like connecting your phone to a wireless device?' Pixel said. 'But what could it be?'

Everyone had stopped what they were doing and stared at the watch. Granny turned off the music. Clíona stood up and swung the beam around the room. The pulses got faster, then slower, then faster again as she swung it towards the fireplace. The beam went solid as it locked onto the oil painting over the fire. The glass of the frame went dark and mathematical formulae started appearing on it.

Clíona gasped. Somehow, the beam was reading the mathematical notes in the glass. 'Look,' she whispered. 'Look at it.'

They were all looking at it. It seemed to be a lot of gibberish.

'It's Alexander's research,' Clíona told them. 'He didn't destroy it all. Somehow, he had it stored in the glass for us, but he couldn't risk McGaffney getting it, so we couldn't unlock it until we brought the watch back here. It's like the watch unlocks it.'

'But what are we supposed to *do* with it?' Onion asked.

'Mum can help us find some scientists who'll know how to use it,' Clíona said. Then she added, 'Though it'll probably take *years* to figure it all out. They can't just go experimenting on old people like Alexander did.'

'The old people didn't seem to mind,' Dallan said.

'Yeah, but there's *laws* about that kind of thing,' Sive said.

CHAPTER TWENTY-FIVE: ONE LAST THING

'Oh, right.'

Onion couldn't make any sense of the code, but he understood what it meant to *have it*. 'So the People in Black lost?' he said.

'Life is a web of incredibly complex interactions,' Clíona replied. 'I don't think we can treat it as a game that's won or lost ...'

'Did McGaffney get what she wanted?'

'No,' Clíona replied.

'And we did?'

'Yes.'

'Well, there you go. We won.'

Onion looked around at the others, and though they were all smiling, for a few moments, nobody knew what to say. Nobody, that was, except Granny.

'Well, since everyone's up on their feet,' she said in a loud voice that made them all jump, 'why don't we all take our places for a foxtrot? Onion, play the music please!'

And for the moment, all thoughts of world-changing developments were put aside so that

some elderly people could dance. Which is just
how it should be sometimes.